FUGITIVE

BOOK FIVE OF THE SHADOW ORDER

MICHAEL ROBERTSON

Email: subscribers@michaelrobertson.co.uk

Edited by:

Terri King - http://terri-king.wix.com/editing
And
Pauline Nolet - http://www.paulinenolet.com

Cover Design by Dusty Crosley

Michael Robertson
© 2017 Michael Robertson

Fugitive - Book five of The Shadow Order is a work of fiction. The
characters, incidents, situations, and all dialogue are entirely a product of
the author's imagination, or are used fictitiously and are not in any way
representative of real people, places or things.

Any resemblance to persons living or dead is entirely coincidental.

CHAPTER 1

Once Seb arrived at the end of the corridor, he leaned against the cold metal of the grey wall. Gunmetal grey, it showed a total lack of aesthetic ambition for the place. Not that it needed to have thick carpets and velvet walls, just something a little less depressing would have been nice. The wall didn't feel unbearably cold to touch, but something about it penetrated his psyche with its stark chill. Bright strip lighting ran along the white ceiling, highlighting his barren surroundings. The fact that he currently had his attention on Moses did little to warm him up.

In front of the simulation rooms, the faces of twenty or so rookies looking at him, Moses walked up and down the line. With wide, confident strides and dramatic arm gestures to show his enthusiasm, he filled their heads with the Shadow Order's bullshit rhetoric.

"The Shadow Order keeps the universe in check," he said. "We save planets, sometimes from outside threats—sometimes from themselves. We're the people others come to when no one else can get the job done."

As Seb watched the large shark-like creature, his stomach

tensed and bile rose in his throat. He tightened his jaw and fought against his urge to go out there and call Moses out on his lies. The Shadow Order existed to line Moses' pockets. To do that, he needed to inspire the next influx of grunts to put their necks on the line for him.

Only small, but firm enough to be uncomfortable in his pocket, Seb absentmindedly fiddled with the dead grub from Carstic. The one Sparks had vomited up in the tank. The creatures had somehow gotten onto the planet. There had to be a way to find out exactly how. Although he couldn't rule them out as indigenous to Carstic, something about their last mission hadn't rung true. He owed it to Wilson and his family to find out for sure, and until he knew the answer, he couldn't do another mission for the Shadow Order.

Seb only heard the footsteps when they were directly behind him. His world slowed down as he spun around, but before he balled his steel fists, he saw her and relaxed. "Sparks?"

"I've been looking for you."

"Well, here I am."

The small Sparks stood no more than three and a half feet tall. It must have been clear to her that Seb had been spying on something. She clung on to him and peered into the training room to see what he was watching.

After a few seconds, Sparks stepped back a pace. Her purple eyes narrowed behind her glasses. She clearly trusted Moses as much as Seb did. "What's he saying to them?"

"The usual crap. It's all about how great the Shadow Order are and how altruistic their intentions."

"He's not mentioned the large amount of credits yet?"

"What do you think?"

When Sparks didn't reply, Seb looked out again. Amongst the rookies he saw the Hispanic woman who'd piloted the mech he'd fought against before their last mission. Moses had called her Reyes. She sat on one of the wooden benches, shoulder to shoulder with what looked to be equally incompetent teenagers and early twenty-somethings. Despite only being a few years younger than him, they looked like kids. Fresh-faced and wet behind the ears. Would Moses have sent Bruke out on a mission with her? Surely he just did it to bait Seb so he would go to Carstic. It had worked too; he couldn't have taken the gamble. What if he'd called his bluff and Bruke had gone out? No way would he have returned if she'd been leading the mission.

"Do you think you'll ever like him?" Sparks said.

"Moses?"

"Who else?"

"No. Do you?"

She shrugged. "We might have to work for him for a *long* time."

"I don't *have* to do anything."

A twisting of Sparks' features showed him she didn't strictly agree with that.

"I'm not anyone's bitch, Sparks."

Sparks raised her hands, showing Seb her palms and long fingers in defence of his aggression. "I didn't say that."

"What are you saying, then?"

"Just that when he needed to get you going out on his behalf last time, he managed to find leverage. He's as cunning as they come and doesn't have a compassionate bone in his body. That will always out trump you because you're better than he is."

"You mean weaker," Seb said. "But not anymore." He turned his back on her. Maybe he'd be able to find peace in the Shadow Order when he found out about the parasite. But he couldn't tell Sparks that. He didn't want her coming with him. It hurt to even think about what he had to do, but he needed to get her away from him. "He might be able to outwit you," Seb said, "but I won't continue to let him keep the upper hand over me."

Sparks scowled and jutted her chin out at him.

"Well?" Seb said. "Listen to yourself. You're talking like I should get used to this life. Like I should cash in and forget about the bigger picture. Like I should sell out. That might come naturally to you, but it certainly doesn't to me." It was hard for him to keep up his mean streak, especially after nearly losing her a couple of days before. He held her glare and bit back his urge to apologise.

Sparks threw her hands up in the air and shook her head at him. "What's got into you today?"

"*You* have. Why do you need to wind me up? I'm tired. I'm still recovering from having to save your life, remember?"

"Is that how this works now?" Sparks said. "We're keeping score?"

"What do you expect? You're trying to tell me a life in Moses' service is the best I can hope for."

"You're really not hearing that well today, are you?"

"Actually, I think I am. You're a button pusher, Sparks. You love a wind-up, but I don't know why you're doing it today. Maybe you feel vulnerable about me saving your arse *again*."

Instead of speaking, Sparks forced her hands against her hips and tilted her head to one side. When she finally opened her mouth to reply—the sound of her inhale running away from them up the hard-surfaced corridor—Seb cut her off. "Don't even try to justify yourself."

Genuine confusion twisted Sparks' face. Hardly surprising because of how unreasonable Seb was being. But he had to be. He had to push her away. "I don't know what's gotten into you today," she finally said.

Seb didn't answer. Instead, he turned his back on his small friend, more to hide his shame about how he'd treated her than anything else. The cold press of the metal wall stretched into his upper arm again as he leaned against it. He listened to Moses' voice echoing through the large space.

"I'm not going to sugarcoat it; every mission will challenge you. Not everyone will come back. But if you're successful—and let me tell you, those who make it back are *always* successful—you can come back here knowing you've made a difference."

Seb shook his head.

"Look," Sparks said.

Seb turned to face her again.

"I really don't understand your mood today. Do you want to tell me what's going on?"

The bright glare of the corridor's strip lighting forced Seb to squint as he stared at her.

"Okay then, *fine!* I'm going to remove myself from this situation. You're clearly pissed off about something and think it's appropriate to take it out on me. All I can do is get out of the line of fire."

As Sparks walked away, Seb watched her small form and let go of a hard sigh. One of the best, if not *the* best, friends he had in the galaxy, and he'd just pushed her away like that. Not just her; he didn't want Bruke or SA coming with him either. He needed to do this alone. He needed to follow his path without dragging them into it.

To think about SA took him back to the desert on Carstic. He'd nearly told her he loved her. The perfect opportunity, maybe he should have. Now he'd have to wait. If he came back to the Shadow Order, he could tell her then. If he didn't make it, it wouldn't be fair to put that on her. She might not care about him at all, but if she did, he didn't want to leave her with the feeling of what could have been. Even then, as he stood there, he felt the press of her lips against his cheek from when they were in the mine. He'd get back to her. He'd get back to all of them. Sparks would forgive him when she understood why he'd pushed her away. At least he hoped she would.

Before Seb went on any more missions for the Shadow Order, he needed to know Wilson's death had nothing to do with them. He needed to know the parasites hadn't been planted on Carstic by his boss. But he needed to do this mission alone. He wouldn't drag his mates into it like he'd dragged them into a war with the Crimson army. He couldn't lose anyone else.

As the bark of Moses' authority rang out through the training area, Seb turned his back on what would soon become his enemy—if only temporarily. Now Sparks had gone from the corridor, he could set off too. Towards his next move. Towards the truth. And most importantly, without his teammates.

CHAPTER 2

Seb reached the other end of the grey corridor, his face hurting from squinting against the glare of the strip lighting. With the jail cell finally in his sights, he took a moment's pause as he tried to centre himself for what he had to do next.

Two guards stood at the door, both of them clearly from the same species as the minotaur Seb had fought beside on Solsans. Unlike the one he'd fought beside, they were both only about eight feet tall; yet they still had broad shoulders and thick arms. They each had two huge curved horns like a Viking's helmet, and large wet black noses that glistened beneath the bright light.

Both of the guards watched Seb as he walked up to them. As hard as he tried, he couldn't prevent his throat from drying, and he had to fight to keep his tone even so he didn't reveal his lie. "Moses sent me down here to get you two."

After a look at one another, one of the guards shrugged. "To do what?"

"You think I'd ask him that? It's none of my business, and I don't care for it to be."

Separated by the width of the prison door as they stood on either side of it—the metal barrier covered in rust but no less resilient for it—the guards looked at one another again.

"He wants *both* of us?" said the one who'd already spoken.

Seb shrugged. Easier to be nonchalant when he didn't speak.

"Who will guard the prison?"

"What do you think he's sent me down here for?"

Another shared look and the vocal guard shook his head. "No."

"It looks to me like you're either calling me a liar, or you're ignoring a direct order from the big man."

"It does seem that way, doesn't it?" Both guards lifted their electric prods ever so slightly, tilting them in Seb's direction, daring him to step closer.

A deep breath pulled Seb's world into slow motion and he saw both creatures' weak spots. They were in the centre of their chests. "Don't say I didn't give you an out," he said.

Before the beasts could react, Seb darted forward and drove one of his metal fists into the centre of the vocal creature's chest. It gasped, the air driven from its lungs in a deep bark.

As the first creature fell, Seb saw the other one swing its electric prod at him and he jumped back. A split second for the creature served as several for him. Time to think. He stared into its dark brown eyes and saw two things: a commitment to its course of action, and fear. It knew it couldn't win, but what would Moses do if it didn't try? However, instead of attacking him again, it looked over his shoulder back down the corridor.

Were it not for the warning, Seb wouldn't have been

aware of his third opponent. It moved quietly enough for him not to hear it over the noise of his current duel.

As the footsteps drew closer, Seb spun around to be faced with a wall of a beast. Over twelve feet tall and covered in orange leathery skin, it looked like Godzilla's little brother.

Even with his world slowed down, Seb had to work on instinct and dropped to the ground to avoid the large leathery beast's electric prod. It seemed odd for it to use that rather than its large fists.

On his way down, Seb saw the minotaur behind him try to grab where he'd been a split second before. It got an electric prod in its chest for its troubles.

A loud buzz, frothy and foaming spittle, and the smell of scorched hair, the brute convulsed with the electric shock before it crumpled to the ground like its pal had. Even with everything else going on, Seb laughed. "Dumb beast."

Seb remained low and saw the orange brute walked on the tips of its toes. A hard swipe with his leg, he took the creature's stability away from it, throwing its feet forwards and sending it falling backwards. The beast's electric prod crashed down at the same time as the creature, adding a buzz to the thud of its large rear connecting with the ground.

Its body not suited for righting itself in a hurry, the creature remained down while Seb seized his opportunity. He jumped to his feet and punched the beast on the snout. It stood out as its weak spot, but the creature remained conscious despite the force of his steel-lined blow.

Seb punched it again, its head thrashing from side to side as it tried to avoid his attack and failed. Four, five, six punches. The brute looked stunned, slowing down a little as it tried to stay away from Seb's blows.

Heavily panting from the fight, sweat running down his

face, and his jaw clenched so tightly the side of his head ached, Seb screamed and put all he had into another punch.

His fist sank into the monster's face and it fell limp.

Gasping, Seb straightened his back and looked up and down the depressing but brightly lit corridor. It looked empty.

The more vocal of the two minotaurs had seemed like the leader, so Seb checked its pockets first. He found the keys for the prison cell on the first time of looking.

A large ring of about thirty keys, Seb's eyes fell to the one with as much rust on it as the door. When he tried it, the lock snapped free with a loud *clunk.*

Another quick check up and down the bright corridor. It looked clear, so Seb pulled the cell door open, the rusty hinges doing their best to give away his movements.

The second Seb stepped into the confined space, the smell drove him back, nearly knocking him over. A sour combination of halitosis and sweat, he had to press the back of his hand to his nose before he stepped forward again.

The prisoners moved away from Seb when he entered. Some of them looked at the dropped guards behind him. Many of the creatures he'd fought the last time he'd been in the cell were still there. The large brown version of Bruke looked at the floor. The crew of seven with the two bat-like creatures all turned away from him. However, the mandulu who ran the place still had the courage to fix him with a dark glare.

To see the swelling on his face made Seb wince, and he dragged a sharp intake of breath as he looked down at the toilet bowl. The dent made by the mandulu's face looked larger than he remembered it. "Sorry about last time, old chap." He laughed. "I had to find a way to stop you from trying to fight me, and I didn't want to kill you."

The mandulu continued to stare. Then, like the minotaur

had done only minutes before, the fat chinned beast looked over Seb's shoulder.

Before Seb had time to react, he heard the crackle of three electric prods behind him. He continued to stare at the mandulu. "I'm guessing someone's still pissed about last time, then?"

CHAPTER 3

Three thugs. All of them the same species. All of them unfamiliar to Seb because they hadn't been there the last time he had. They moved in on him like they'd done this before. They worked as a team. One directly in front of him and one to either side. They were all shorter than him, but even the narrowest of the three had at least an extra thirty centimetres width than he did. The largest had the proportions of a square. Pink-skinned like hairless moles, they looked built for strength. Their small brow-less heads suggested they didn't have much space for brains.

They might have been unfamiliar to Seb, but he was unfamiliar to them too. Maybe that was why they were prepared to attack him.

Looking into their vacant stares, Seb watched their brilliant blue eyes for some form of cognition. When he didn't see it, he smiled to himself. They looked like the perfect henchmen. Just point them where you wanted them to go and they'd attack. The mandulu clearly had something to do with their aggression towards him.

After one final look at the three faces, Seb did what he had to do. A deep breath to centre himself and his world slowed down. He balled his cold metal fists and clenched his jaw.

But before he could step forward, two huge brown arms came around him from behind and clamped across his chest. He shook and twisted, but he couldn't move.

The faces of the three thugs lit up as one. A moment of panic surged through Seb, kicking his pulse up a notch.

No time to think, Seb fell limp. He had enough body-weight to destabilise the brown creature behind him and it came forwards with his fall. Before the beast could recover, Seb kicked off the ground, going against their collective momentum and crashing back up against the brute's face with a wet *clomp.*

What felt like the brute's teeth sent fire through the top of Seb's head. Although he must have done more damage to it because the creature fell away from him, releasing its grip as it toppled backwards. A second later, it hit the ground with a *thump.*

No time to check if it had been knocked out or not, Seb looked at the large round stomachs of the three aggressors in front of him. Their clear weak spot. Most creatures fell from a blow to the face, but these things looked like they had skulls as thick as rock. To punch them there would only hurt him, even with no feeling in his hands.

A slow motion perspective helped Seb see the first swing from a mile away. A measure of its stupidity, the creature used the electric prod as a bat. It must have thought the steel body of the pole would somehow be more effective than the flickering blue electricity on the end of it.

Seb dropped down beneath the attack and punched the idiot in the stomach.

The blow drove the air from the first brute in a deep wheeze, and it folded over as it fell to the floor.

Seb remained low and sent two quick punches into the guts of the other two. Both of them fell like the first had. They slowly flopped forward at the waist and were rendered utterly ineffective.

Before Seb got to his feet, his perspective sped up again. The electric prods lay on the floor, buzzing from where they remained on. They existed as the only sound in the cell, and when he looked around at the other prisoners, wide eyes regarded him as if they feared he'd go for them next.

The brown creature Seb had shrugged off remained down, blood running from its mouth. Seb reached up to the top of his head and felt the lump from where the thing's teeth had connected with his skull.

It took a few seconds for Seb's breathing to settle from the effort of the fight. For that time, he felt the attention of the room on him. He then focused on the mandulu in the corner.

The mandulu stared back.

"You may have had something to do with what just happened."

When the mandulu opened its mouth to reply, he cut it off. "I don't care if you did. In fact, I don't want to know. You're free to go," Seb said.

If not the entire room, then a large majority of them gasped at his comment.

"*What?*" the mandulu said.

"I'm setting you free. All of you. It's not that hard to get your head around, is it?"

A glance at the three knocked-out brutes, Seb laughed. "They gave me a workout, that's all. They weren't a serious threat in any way. Oh, and when you leave, I don't want any harm to come to the guards outside. They're as much a victim of Moses' insanity as you all are. I know screws and prisoners don't get on, but they're just doing their job. I don't want them punished for that."

"Are you aware of how they treated us?" the mandulu said.

Seb pulled his head back. "I'm sorry, did I give off the impression that this was a discussion?"

Silence.

"Right. Now get out of here before I change my mind."

Although Seb waited, none of the prisoners moved.

When Seb looked around the room at them, they all dropped their attention to their feet. "I'm going to leave the door open. I'm not going to hold your hands. You decide if you want to leave or not." He fought to hide the panic in his voice. The plan wouldn't work if they didn't leave. He needed the chaos of a prison break.

Seb then saw the grey creature. Although he'd seen it the last time he'd been in the prison, he got to truly take it in now. It stood about five feet six inches tall and looked like a rock troll with its granite eyes and skin. It had long coarse black hair that looked almost synthetic. The stocky thing had a frame somewhere between a human and a gorilla. Broad shoulders, a slight hunch to its stance, long and powerful arms. After finally pointing at it, he said, "You! You're coming with me."

The rock troll clearly didn't need a second invitation. It as good as ran towards Seb at his request. It must have made him unpopular when he'd called Seb the chosen one because he appeared desperate to get out of there.

Anxiety twisted through Seb to see the others still hadn't moved. What would it take to get chaos streaming out of the cell?

Once outside—the three guards still out cold—Seb

grabbed the rock troll's arm and dragged it around the corner. Despite the bright lights, he found a shadowy spot and pressed against the cold steel wall.

Although it followed Seb's lead, the grey creature looked confused. "What are we doing?" it asked in a whisper.

Seb peered around the corner and said, "Waiting."

"For what?"

Suddenly, the prisoners ran from the cell, and some of the tension left Seb's frame. A stampede, they moved as one, all of them heading away in the opposite direction.

Seb watched them for a moment before he said, "That."

When enough of the prisoners had left the cell, Seb reached over for the red alarm button on the wall and smashed his fist against it. A loud screeching siren soared through the long corridors and no doubt the rest of the complex too. So shrill, it threw Seb's balance off. He shouted at the grey creature, "We need Moses focusing on anything but us at this point."

The creature nodded.

"It helps that they attacked me."

"Why?"

"It takes some of the guilt away. They're all about to run into a room full of Shadow Order cadets. They may only be young, but all of them are trained and keen. The prisoners don't stand a chance against them. It'll buy us the time we need to get out of here."

The shrill alarm bored into Seb and wound his shoulders tight. "Come on"—he pointed up as if to indicate the sound around them—"let's get out of here before my brain melts."

Seb set off in the opposite direction to all of the prisoners. The rock troll followed.

"Where are we going?" the grey creature asked.

After he'd crossed the corridor and opened a door, Seb

revealed a metal staircase. "Where would you go if you wanted to get out of here?" He stepped through into the cold concrete maintenance area. It smelled of damp, salty damp, because of their position beneath the sea. Seb crinkled his nose at the stench.

"Most beings would go to the platform up top."

"Exactly." After the grey creature had stepped through, Seb closed the door and headed down the stairs. "That's why we're heading in the opposite direction."

The red emergency lighting made it trickier to navigate their descent. For the first time, Seb missed the magnesium glare of the lights in the corridor. The crimson glow pulsed in time with the dizzying sound of the alarm. His stomach lurched with every step, his vision so poor he feared he might fall.

But Seb soon found his rhythm, gripping the cold and damp handrail as he ran down the stairs two at a time towards the basement. The thud of the troll's steps followed behind him—it didn't have a problem keeping up.

They only had to descend a couple of floors, but when the door to the basement came into sight, Seb halted and let out a heavy sigh. "Damn!"

"What?" the grey creature asked as it caught up to him, breathless from their run.

"I left the guard's keys in the prison cell. We can't get through that door."

Before Seb could think on it, the grey creature grabbed him and pulled him into the shadows. The door in front of them clicked and flew open. Three guards burst through it.

"Moses wants everyone to go to the landing platform," one of them said as they ran past Seb and the troll.

The others followed him up the stairs, and within seconds they were out of sight.

Before Seb could think, the grey creature darted forwards and caught the door, preventing it from clicking shut.

Seb laughed. "It's not often I feel like I'm a step behind."

A stoic nod, the rock troll pulled the door wide, the green glow of the basement spilling out into the red stairwell.

Seb stepped into the space and gasped. It looked like an aquarium. A large window ran the entire length of one wall. It revealed the weird and wonderful aquatic life of Aloo. Not that he had time to admire the view; the alarm still pulsed through the room, reminding him they needed to get out of there now.

"I'm glad we came down here," the grey creature said.

Seb looked to where he looked. In one corner sat a bay filled with all different kinds of vessels. It suddenly dawned on him what the troll had said when they'd entered the stairwell. "You said most beings would go to the platform up top, but you didn't say *you* would."

The troll's granite eyes glowed as if it had just seen an old friend. "That's my submarine over there."

"I was thinking I'd have to drive one of those things. Are you saying you can get us out of here?"

The rock troll broke into a jog towards his sub. "You betcha I can."

CHAPTER 4

The whir of the submarine's engines vibrated through the small vessel. For the first part of their journey, Seb twisted in his seat and looked over his shoulder behind him through the glass roof. He waited until darkness swallowed the Shadow Order's base before he looked anywhere else.

Designed for beings smaller than him, Seb had to stoop because of the low ceiling. Although uncomfortable, he had enough movement to take in his surroundings. Above him, the water turned slightly lighter from the sun trying to penetrate the gloomy depths. To the sides and below, it plunged into inky blackness within a few short metres. The submarine's beam did little to help.

A clear panel by his feet, Seb looked down again. Unable to ascertain just how far the depths plunged, his stomach flipped. He'd never liked the water, but now he had metal fists, he liked it even less.

If the deep frown on its face was anything to go by, the troll clearly needed to concentrate, but Seb still spoke, his anxiety driving his words. "I know I spend a lot of time in space, but there's something about the sea. If the engines fail now, it looks like we'd drop forever."

At that moment the rock troll threw the submarine to the left and Seb grabbed onto his seat, his heart jumping into his throat.

The rock troll didn't look back when Seb stared at him, so he looked over his shoulder and saw what they'd avoided. The tentacle appeared to be like many he'd seen: covered in suckers, thick, and as black as the night. However, he'd never seen one so large. They'd only avoided the tip of it. A tip that would have wrecked them if it had made contact. Another look down into the darkness and he squirmed in his seat. "How long till we're on shore?"

The troll said nothing as the sub wobbled from side to side, the water disturbed by the great tentacle's movement. Seb watched it vanish back into the depths behind them. "What was that thing?"

No sign of nerves, the grey creature fought to keep the sub level and continued to stare out of the windscreen into the darkness in front of them. "I don't know."

"You've never seen one before?"

"I've seen plenty of those tentacles before."

Another look down showed the darkness as black and impenetrable as it was moments before. Seb shook his head. "Better that than see what was on the end of it, I suppose."

"Exactly."

It took another few seconds for Seb to settle himself. His body remained tense and his pulse rapid. "I suppose the water stresses me out now because of how I swim with my new fists."

No response. And what could his new friend say to that? He knew nothing of Seb's fists and it would take too long to explain. "I've just realised," Seb said, "I never asked your name."

The creature smiled, its granite eyes focused in front of it still. "No, you didn't."

"Well? What is it?"

"Owsk."

"Owsk?"

"Owsk."

Seb shifted to try to find more comfort in his cramped seat. "Well, I'm pleased to meet you. I'm Seb."

"I know that."

"Of course you do. So, tell me, what do you know about the prophecy?"

Owsk continued to stare ahead of them, the sub's single thick beam of light giving them just a few more metres visibility than no light at all would. "Not a lot really. Something came over me when I saw you and I knew I needed to say it. You have the blood in your veins of the chosen one. I can feel it. I can sense you have a greatness waiting to be unlocked. That you'll take down the void threatening to consume the galaxy."

"The void?"

Owsk shrugged.

"Well, that's answered all of my questions. Thanks."

After a few seconds of silence, Owsk finally said, "I didn't say I could answer your questions."

Owsk then dropped the sub by a few metres, leaving Seb's stomach where it had been moments before. He looked up to watch them pass beneath a large brown fish easily three times the size of their vessel. It moved with lazy strokes of its huge fins. It seemed to be scanning its surroundings despite its milky white eyes on its ugly face.

To look at its size set Seb's panic off again and he

muttered to himself, "In the land of the blind, the photosensitive are king."

"Huh?" Owsk said.

"Nothing."

Owsk shrugged. "So what are you doing breaking out of the Shadow Order's base?"

The cramped conditions forced Seb to straighten his right leg so he could access his pocket. He slipped two fingers into it and retrieved the hard little parasite Sparks had thrown up in the tank.

For the first time since they'd left the Shadow Order's base, Owsk took his attention away from the darkness in front of them and looked at Seb, or rather, the grub in his pinch. He frowned. "What's *that*?"

"A lot of people died on Carstic, which is where our last mission was. They died because of *this* parasite."

When Owsk didn't respond, Seb elaborated. "We only found three survivors in the entire mining complex. One of them theorised that these grubs were planted on their planet to clear the mines."

"Why?"

"They mine for ruthane, and ruthane's worth a lot of credits."

A shrug, Owsk said, "There has to be more to it than that. There's not always a conspiracy when there's credits involved."

"Before the survivors—who were quite vocal about their theory, I might add—could get off the planet, their ship blew up."

"Oh."

"Yeah," Seb said. "*Oh*."

"And you think Moses has something to do with it?"

"Well, Moses certainly got paid from the people who

owned the mines. They had to bring in the Shadow Order to clear them out. They'd also just recently paid the Shadow Order to rescue their incompetent son from Solsans, so he knew their credits were good."

A deep sigh and Owsk said, "You think Moses is exploiting them for their wealth?"

"I think so, but I don't have the evidence to prove it."

"So what will you do if you find out Moses is responsible for planting the parasites?"

For a second, Seb said nothing. Instead, he stared out into the darkness and chewed on his bottom lip. The whir of the submarine's engine continued to shake through him as he drew a deep breath of the odourless air. "I don't know," he finally said. "He's powerful and is going to be hard to get to if he knows I'm coming for him."

"And you think he'll know?"

"Well, I'm a fugitive now, so if I come back, it probably won't be for a friendly reunion."

"I suppose. Where are the others?" Owsk said. "Your friends?"

To think about how mean he had been to Sparks twisted through Seb. And he hadn't said goodbye to Bruke. The kiss on the cheek from SA might be the only one he'd ever get from her. A feeling of bleakness settled over him and his breaths grew shallow. He'd be without them when he needed them most. It took him a second to compose himself. "I don't want them with me." Then Gurt came to mind and the tension in his chest eased a little. He'd made the correct choice. "They shouldn't get themselves screwed over because I'm chasing a hunch. A friend of mine died following me into a war when I didn't want him to."

"And they'd do the same?" Owsk asked.

"They did, and they would again."

"So you didn't give them the choice?"

"No."

"You think that's your decision, do you?"

A snap of fury spiked through Seb and he looked across at Owsk. Who did he think he was? "Of *course*!" Then he thought about how cross the others had been with him in the mines. They hadn't been happy with the decisions he'd made on their behalf, especially with how he'd completely disregarded SA and her abilities. Yet now he was doing it again.

A look at Owsk and the granite appraisal the creature levelled on him, Seb clenched his jaw, speaking through gritted teeth. "Anyway," he said, trying to move the conversation away from Owsk's opinions of his actions, "what's *your* deal?"

The sharpness of his tone forced Owsk to pull his head back and he returned his attention to the thick wall of water in front of them. They passed through a school of bioluminescent fish, traces of glowing blue phosphoresce left behind when they scattered. In the extreme glow, he saw SA's eyes. He felt the warm memory of her kiss.

Seb moved on and softened his tone. "Sorry, that came out wrong. It's just ... I didn't know about the Shadow Order's prison until I was in it. How did you end up in there?"

Owsk made another sharp turn to avoid another whale of a fish. Seb held on again, already getting used to the sudden changes in direction.

"Moses runs Aloo, right?" Owsk said.

A shrug, Seb nodded. "Yeah, it certainly seems that way."

"Everyone knows that contraband passes through the spaceport on a daily basis."

"Yeah, of course. Aloo's renowned for giving smugglers

an easy ride. So what did you do that would land you in jail on a planet that actively encourages criminal activity?"

This time Owsk pulled back on his controls and the ship rose. It went over the next creature, a green eel ten times the length of the sub. "I was only smuggling exotic fruit."

"That doesn't sound like a big deal."

"The duty on it's *huge*. They like to hammer you on anything with a short shelf life because you don't have the time to negotiate. Also, they fetch big prices in the right places, so they know you'll make the credits back. We were trying to avoid that, which is why we went through Aloo."

"Okay."

"But we couldn't afford to pay Moses his fee either."

"Ah! So you were looking for a free ride from the galaxy's tightest being?"

"Not a free ride. We promised it to him on the way back, but it would seem the bank of Aloo aren't into credit. He threw me in jail until one of my crew could pay."

"And they haven't?"

"Not yet. They've impounded our ship, so we can't sell our stock. And we can't make credits on Aloo to pay him back."

"Tell me about it. Unless you know how to fight, Aloo's got pretty slim pickings."

"Exactly." While holding out one of his thick arms, Owsk said, "We may look strong, but we're pacifists. You wouldn't ever catch a jelk in a fighting pit; we've not got it in us."

"And when we get to Aloo's spaceport, you can leave without any trouble?"

"As long as my ship flies, we'll work out a way." A slight pause, the hum of the engine filling the silence, Owsk then said, "Also, I might be able to help you with that grub."

"Oh?"

"I know a creature that can trace anything to its origin. He makes a killing in finding slaves and charging their loved ones to get them back to them."

"He sounds like a kidnapper."

"No, he takes them *back* from the kidnappers. He lets the families pay in instalments for as long as they need to."

"My bad." Seb rolled his eyes and couldn't keep the sarcasm from his voice. "He sounds like a saint."

For the first time since they'd been together, Owsk laughed. A deep, stuttering sound, it bounced off the glass surfaces inside the ship. "Yeah, he's definitely in it for himself, but at least he's quite reasonable about collecting his credits. He'll never hold out on reuniting someone with their loved ones. Anyway, he owes me a few favours from when I've helped move beings around for him. I can ask him to help you."

Before Seb could respond, Owsk pulled back on the submarine's controls, harder than before. It sent them shooting towards the surface.

With nothing to hold onto, Seb braced against the glass window next to him and watched the water get rapidly lighter.

The aggressive change from the dark sea to the bright Aloo sunshine stung Seb's eyes as they burst through the surface of the water. He shielded them for a few seconds and waited for his sight to return while they floated with the undulations of the choppy sea.

A press of a button, Owsk then looked up as the glass top of the submarine pulled back. It let in the salty Aloo air, the wind throwing Seb's hair into his eyes.

Owsk jumped out of the submarine first and held a hand out in Seb's direction. Seb took it and stepped out onto land, trying not to look down. One slip and he'd sink faster than a rock. When he walked away, his first few steps were uneasy from still having his sea legs.

Once clear of the vessel, Seb and Owsk stepped back a few paces from it. Before either of them spoke, Seb pulled out his blaster and ripped off several shots, his gun kicking as the laser fire drilled holes through the sub's open cockpit.

Horror turned Owsk's face slack as he looked from his sub, to Seb, and back to his sub again. Water sprouted from the fresh holes, driven a few metres into the air from the force of his sinking ship.

"What was that for?" Owsk said.

"I guarantee it had a tracker in it." Seb continued to watch the water as the vessel vanished from sight. "The second they realise the sub has gone missing, they'll track it down. When they realise where it is, they'll think we sank with it. We need as much time as possible."

When Owsk didn't respond, Seb turned to look at him, bracing against the strong Aloo winds as he did so. To see the end of a gun pointed in his direction sent panic spiking through him. "What are you doing?"

Tears sat in Owsk's granite eyes and he spoke through gritted teeth. "What do you mean *what am I doing?* You just *destroyed* my ship."

CHAPTER 5

"Now calm down," Seb said, his voice raised over the strong wind crashing into them. He'd slipped his gun down the back of his trousers after he'd shot the submarine, and although he could have drawn it, he didn't need to escalate the situation. Not yet.

The tears in Owsk's eyes had thickened and looked like they'd spill over. Wrinkles ran across his granite brow like cracks in rock. "*Calm down*? You've just shot my submarine full of holes and sunk it. What do you mean *calm down*?"

Salt rode the strong breeze, making it burn against Seb's face. "Would you rather I left it there so Moses could find us? I guarantee you there's a tracking device in it."

Still with his gun trained on Seb, Owsk said, "You could have said."

"I *did*."

"*Before* you shot it. I can remove a tracking device. I can't replace that submarine."

A look to where the vessel had only just been, the sea crashing over the edge of the rocks as the waves broke against them, Seb scoffed a laugh. "It can't have been worth that much. It was ancient."

Owsk closed the distance between them in just two strides. He pushed the cold steel barrel of his gun so hard against Seb's temple it sent the start of a headache streaking through his eyes.

The act of aggression slowed down Seb's world, but he held his position, pushing his head back against Owsk's pressure despite the pain of it. With slow and deliberate words, he spoke through gritted teeth. "You helped me get away from the Shadow Order's base, so I'll allow you this indiscretion. However, if you don't take your gun away from the side of my head, I'm going to take it off you and shove it so far up your arse you'll feel the barrel against the roof of your mouth."

A wobble ran through the hard weapon, shaking Seb's vision as he waited for Owsk to act. Not prompt enough, he said, "I'll give you to the count of three."

But before Seb could start his countdown, Owsk lowered his gun and sighed.

To look at the thickset granite creature, his arms hanging down by his sides, his shoulders slumped, sent sadness twisting through Seb. In any other situation he would have sparked him, but something didn't seem right. "I'll be honest, it seems like an extreme reaction over a crappy boat."

"Say it again," Owsk said, the wind so strong it even tugged on his heavy hair. He looked at Seb, tears running down his face. "Say that about my submarine again and you'll be wishing you hadn't."

Seb stepped back in the face of Owsk's aggression. He had to remember that Owsk had gotten him away from Moses. Whatever his reason for being so angry, he needed his chance to speak. After drawing a breath to rein in his reaction, Seb said, "Let's start again. *Why* is that boat so important to you?"

For a second, Owsk said nothing. He then put his gun away and sighed. The anger gave way to a grief that twisted his granite face. When he spoke, his mouth buckled. "It's been in my family for centuries. Passed down from father to son for as long as we can remember. We've always smuggled goods through the galaxy, and that submarine has been with us through a lot of scrapes. If you can get to places via land and sea, you get a lot more work. Although the advantages of the sub are much less important than what it meant to me every time I sat in the cockpit. Of the pride I felt for continuing to be good at what we did." His voice broke when he said, "We could have removed the tracker."

Owsk's sadness affected Seb much more than his anger had. When a particularly strong gust of wind clattered into him, he stumbled a few steps to the side. "I'm sorry. I truly am."

After he'd inhaled another deep breath, Owsk pulled his shoulders back and glared at Seb. "Sorry won't get it back."

"Maybe we could—"

"It's at the *bottom* of the sea, Seb. You've seen what's down there."

Although Seb opened his mouth to reply, nothing came out. The taste of salt lay along his tongue when he closed it again. What could he say to that? "So where does that leave us?"

"There is no *us*, Seb. There's just you, me, and the prophecy."

Seb waited for him to continue.

"I'll help you. I'll help you because I believe in the prophecy. Because this is bigger than me and I'm not going to stand in the way of it." Owsk's voice dropped to a growl, his brow set, his eyes deader than they were only moments ago. "But know this, I *hate* you for what you've done. I hate you with everything in me."

They'd been in the strong wind long enough for Seb to be locked tight because of the cold battering. The salty air burned the corners of his eyes, tautening the skin on his face. In a poorly judged attempt to lighten the mood, Seb laughed. "I'll take it."

Muted and stony rage came back at him.

The dead parasite in his pinch, Seb showed it to Owsk as he shrugged. "Let's go find this saint of yours, yeah?"

Owsk paused for a few more seconds before he finally turned his back on Seb and walked off in the direction of Aloo's spaceport.

CHAPTER 6

Seb took the hint and walked a few paces behind Owsk as he strode ahead of him into the spaceport. Purposeful in his gait, every kilo of the granite beast slammed down against the spaceport's ground as if he stamped out his frustration.

Before Seb followed him around the first corner, he looked behind them one last time. Not really at the space where the submarine had been, just behind in general. Something felt amiss. It felt like they were being followed. Yet he only saw the rolling sea. The cold and sharp wind crashed into him as he watched the waves rise and fall. A shake of his head, he then entered the spaceport, moving into the bustling crowd filled with creatures he didn't recognise from planets he'd probably never heard of.

Owsk moved as if he were telepathic, navigating the throng like he could read their next steps. The spaceport looked the same as the last time Seb had visited it. Full of beings, they all rushed in different directions. Heads down, heavy scowls, and no acknowledgement when they bumped into one another. No idea where Owsk was leading him at that moment, he had little choice but to trust him.

Even though Seb and Owsk had several metres separating them, he still felt the tension coming from the rock troll. Those close by seemed to pick up on it too. When they looked at Seb, he saw eyes widening and then narrowing as they recognised what he was: a human! If Owsk was setting him up and sides needed to be picked, their reactions served as a clear display of their allegiance.

The stares did little to help ease Seb's paranoia. He'd walked into the crowd knowing they wouldn't react well to him. On top of that, he hadn't shaken the feeling of being followed. A check behind showed him abundant hostility, but if one of the creatures in the crowd was following him, he had no way of picking them out. At some point Moses would put a bounty on his head, but surely that hadn't happened yet.

Whereas Owsk walked through the press of bodies with ease, Seb met much more resistance. At over twelve feet tall, an ape-like creature walked towards him and stopped directly in his path. Huge hands on its wide hips, it stared down at him.

But Seb didn't react. Instead, he viewed the world in slow motion, which made it easy to skirt around the brute, moving at the last moment to prevent the creature from blocking him again. While he passed him, the brute released a sharp shot of air from its snout, the sweaty halitosis reek of its breath pushing down on the top of Seb's head.

The beast's weak spot stood out from a mile away: a point beneath its right arm. Seb could have dropped it in front of everyone. Maybe they would have backed off, but he and Owsk didn't need any more attention on them. If he started trouble, it would get straight back to Moses.

Several creatures that looked like ants but were the size of large dogs carried crates on their backs. They dumped them in Seb's path. Again, Seb didn't react; instead he stepped on one of the crates, transitioned to the back of one of the ants, and continued after Owsk as if his path had been clear all along. A collective clicking hiss followed him, but none of the ants did any more than that.

Spaceships lined either side of the walkway. Many of them had crew members standing guard outside, and all of them had their cargo doors wide open. They would usually hide their cargo, even on Aloo, but the fact they were open suggested they were yet to collect what they'd come for. Nothing stayed on Aloo for long if it didn't have to. Seb planned to follow that mindset too.

The feeling of being followed still played on Seb, and he turned to look over his shoulder again. He saw nothing other than the collective hostility of the spaceport, yet the unease wouldn't leave him alone. In his gut he knew there was something more than what he'd seen so far. As much as he wished it not to be true, he knew Moses played some part in it.

Thinking of the one large brute that had blocked his way, he turned back around to see a wall of them in front of him now. Smaller than the ape, the six creatures still stood like sentries. In any other situation, he would have fought them if he had to, but he needed to keep his head down and follow Owsk.

Hairy, barrel chested, and with a strong stance, the creatures created what appeared to be an impenetrable wall. But Seb dropped his head, picked up his pace, and headed for the largest of the lot. Take the big one down and the others backed off. At least, they usually did.

When Seb barged into the creature, it took more force than he'd anticipated, but it stumbled enough for him to push his way through.

What sounded like war cries came after Seb, but he ignored them and looked for Owsk. He couldn't see him. A look left and right, his heart quickened. He couldn't see the creature anywhere.

When Seb turned around to look at the beasts that had tried to block his way, he saw them bristle and move close to him again. Owsk had set him up. The hostility around him seemed like much more than that now. Every creature in Aloo was in on it. Moses had already put the call out. He'd been set up. A deep breath, he swallowed a dry gulp and clenched his fists. If he had to go down, he'd fight until he had nothing left to give.

CHAPTER 7

One last check around, Seb first looked left. He saw a bank of ships like all of the others he'd passed so far. A mismatched collection from tiny shuttles to intergalactic freighters. He looked back at the crowd and their anger. No way would he win this fight; he had to try to escape. The beasts he'd shoved past moved a step closer to him.

When Seb looked right at the largest ship he'd seen in the port—chrome and glistening in the strong Aloo sunshine—he suddenly saw the space next to it. A walkway of sorts, he quickened his pace to see into it.

Owsk had made it halfway down the path already, his long black hair hanging between his broad shoulders. The hostility around him suddenly looked very different. Less like a collective agenda. He broke into a jog to catch up with the troll, throwing another check behind him as he ducked into the alleyway. Still no evidence of something following them. Just a mob that hated humans, and a feeling of being watched.

By the time Seb had caught up with Owsk, they were on the other side of the ships. The damp concrete ground stretched away in front of them all the way to the sea. The wind ran stronger than it had in the spaceport, and he blinked against its saline sting, trying to swallow as the salt in the air dried his throat.

In the middle of the expanse of open concrete stood a large warehouse. No other buildings around, it had a chain-link fence surrounding it. Where the spaceport had been hostile, what he now faced looked positively volatile. "Where are we going?" Seb said.

But Owsk didn't reply.

The world in front of Seb still moved in slow motion. He looked behind him at the ships they'd just passed through. Nothing followed them. "Owsk, why do I get the sense that we're walking into a dodgy situation? I thought you were going to take me to your friend. What is this place?"

Still nothing from Owsk. The thickset grey creature increased his pace. Maybe Seb should have turned around at that point. Instead, he broke into a half jog to catch up with his guide.

Seb saw a locked gate in the chain-link fence. When they got a few steps closer, a guard appeared on the other side of it. It had clearly been aware of their approach. A mandulu, it had a semi-automatic blaster strung across its chest. It stared at Owsk and Seb whilst gripping its weapon.

Seb couldn't control his quickening breaths or tightening stomach, but he could control his actions. Until he had a reason to fight, he had to hold back and let everything play out as it needed to. Owsk was pissed with him, but he'd had no tangible reason to doubt him so far.

The mandulu—larger than many Seb had seen at easily nine feet tall—kept one hand on its blaster before pulling the lock on the chain-link gate free with a snap. The hinges creaked as it pulled it open, a heavy glare still on the beast's face.

Although Owsk strolled straight through the gate without breaking stride, Seb stopped. He stared at the mandulu, and the mandulu stared back. The weakness of its fat chin stood out and he balled his metal hands. He could knock it out if it attacked him, but he couldn't let his paranoia win. Also, what lay beyond the gate? And how many other opportunities for help would he come across if he didn't follow Owsk at that moment?

As he watched Owsk walk around the side of the warehouse out of sight and into the unknown, Seb chewed on his bottom lip. A look behind and he still didn't see the presence he'd felt watching him.

After he'd straightened his frame, Seb nodded to himself and walked through the gate. Hopefully Owsk could be trusted.

The mandulu stared at Seb for the entire time, looking down on him as he walked past. Although Seb kept his fists balled, he didn't react. He had to let this play out.

Once he'd gone a few metres past the creature, the rattling slam of the closing gate made Seb jump. But he didn't look around. Don't show them any weakness they can exploit. Just be ready if he needed to be.

On the same path Owsk had walked, Seb rounded the corner to see the warehouse's entrance sat wide open. A metal shutter had been rolled all the way to the top.

The loud wind had masked the sounds from inside the building. Even if Seb had heard the rattling of chains, he would have put it down to the fence outside. But now he saw the creature, he froze. He should have twigged sooner.

A small brown porcupine-looking beast shook and twisted, but it had been wrapped so tightly in heavy metal chains, it couldn't squirm free. A ball gag had been wedged into its mouth and its eyes were wide with fear. Tears had darkened and flattened two vertical lines of fur down its face. What little light they had in the warehouse caught the glistening tracks of the creature's wounds all over its face. It looked like something had gone to town on it with a knife. The creature kept looking down at a pit in the ground.

Six mandulus stood around it, daring it to try something stupid. In the middle of them stood what must have been their boss.

A lizard creature that changed colour from blue to green as the light hit its moving form. It had a thick barbed tail and yellow eyes that were narrowed into tight slits. It might have only been about five feet tall, but it looked like what it lacked in height, it made up for with malice.

Before Seb could do anything, the reptile looked over at him, appraising him with its cold glare. It then pushed its prisoner into the hole in front of it.

It had been hard to tell what lay in the pit until Seb heard the splash as the small chained creature vanished from sight.

"No," Seb said, shaking his head, his breaths quickening. He then looked at Owsk, who'd taken his place beside the mob. Seb pointed to where the porcupine had just gone. "I know you're pissed at me, but I ain't going in there. No way."

But when Seb backed away from the gang, he hit the wall of the mandulu who'd let them in. The press of the guard's blaster felt cold against the base of Seb's skull, and it spoke in a deep voice. "You ain't going anywhere, sunshine."

CHAPTER 8

Usually a creature of impulse, Seb had been about as patient as he could. He should have trusted his instinct and turned around the second he saw the warehouse. He stared into Owsk's granite eyes, and Owsk stared a cold disregard back at him. Whatever he'd done to the dumb creature's submarine, he didn't deserve this. A shake of his head at the granite troll. He did it ever so slightly so as not to startle the mandulu behind him. If he gave him any excuse to pull the trigger, he'd be watching his brains exit through his nose.

As much as Seb wanted to move—even to dip his head to ease the pressure of the cold steel at the base of his skull—he didn't. Instead, he retreated into his gift, the world slowing down around him.

Probably imperceptible at a normal speed, Seb felt the slightest easing of pressure on the back of his head. He didn't need any more encouragement than that.

Dropping to the hard concrete ground, Seb looked up as he fell to see a pulse of red laser fire shoot over the top of him. If he hadn't moved, would the creature have blown his brains out, or did the movement panic it into pulling the trigger?

Before the mandulu had time to react to him not being there, Seb spun around and swept its legs from beneath it. He connected clean, a loud and satisfying *crack* ringing out before the beast's feet flew skywards. The ground shook when the lump of a brute landed hard on its back.

Over it in a flash, Seb punched the creature. The connection ran through the brute's fat chin, sending ripples across its chubby face and turning its lights off.

By the time he'd gotten to his feet, Seb looked across the warehouse to see the six mandulus that had been by the hole charging his way. The lizard creature ran in the opposite direction—probably to hide, if it had any sense.

They came forward as a pack, a wall of mandulu. But Seb had been here before. He had all the time in the world to watch their slow charge. So long, in fact, he snapped his neck from side to side, balled his fists, and smiled at the attack. None of them were armed. This would be a walk in the park.

Giddy with anticipation, adrenaline lighting him up, Seb roared when the creatures got closer.

Then he heard it.

Snap!

When Seb looked in the direction of the sound, he saw a wall of chain flying towards him. It didn't matter that he saw it in slow motion because it moved so fast and stretched so wide, he couldn't avoid the metal net's spread.

Just before he took the impact, Seb saw the lizard through the net. It stood by a large cannon it had obviously used to fire it from.

Too much time to think, his breaths quickening, his heart racing, Seb almost welcomed the violent embrace just to stop the anticipation of it. The heavy metal chains—each link as thick as a mandulu's finger—crashed into him, gathered him up like he weighed nothing, and squeezed the air from his lungs. The smell of metal surrounded him as he got scrunched into a ball. The momentum of the net dragged him out of the warehouse into the dock beyond. A loud *whoosh* filled his ears as the chains scraped over the concrete ground.

The cold links of the net pressed against Seb's face, making it hard for him to see. Not that he needed to be a genius to identify the six large forms descending on him.

Seb's bonds allowed him the slightest twist before they locked him tight again. He'd moved enough, however, to be able to see the blaster nearby. It must have been the one the mandulu had pressed to the back of his neck. He'd obviously dragged it with him when he got caught up in the net. As much as he fought to be free of his bonds, he couldn't untangle himself. Thick, heavy webbing—the more he struggled, the more it crushed him in its grip.

Still partially blinded by the chains pressed against his face, Seb could have sworn he saw a figure move around the side of the warehouse. Clearly nothing to do with the lizard creature and his henchmen, they looked to be hiding. As much as he tried to angle his head to see better, he couldn't. It had to have something to do with Moses.

In real time, the mandulus would have closed down on Seb in seconds. It felt like minutes as he waited for them to get near.

"You lot are brave, aren't you?" Seb said as he tried to twist and shake against his bonds.

The mandulus closed in a little more, blocking out the bright Aloo sunshine.

"I wish I had the courage of you lot. I mean, it takes a fierce warrior to approach someone wrapped up in chains on the ground. Especially when they have five of their friends with them to hold their hands."

"Shut up," one of the mandulus said.

A shake of his head, his breaths running away from him, his pulse rampaging, Seb said, "You were just about to get your arses kicked. If I walk away from this, I promise you, I won't forget I owe you a whoppin'."

Before Seb could say anything else, he saw one of the mandulus lean over him and raise its fist. Telegraphed from a mile away, he could do nothing but wait for the inevitable sting as its punch forced the thick chains hard against his nose. A nauseating crack ran through Seb's face and he instantly tasted the metallic tang of his own blood.

Another blow flashed white light through Seb's right eye, and the sting lit up the side of his face like an electric shock. His head moved from side to side as several more blows crashed into him, each one fogging his perspective and slowly turning the daylight surrounding him to darkness.

CHAPTER 9

Every muscle in Seb's body ached when he came to, but most of the pain sat in his face. The swelling felt like he had knots of fire beneath his skin. Whenever he moved, electric shocks streaked through his sinuses and jabbed knives into his eyes. Hardly surprising when he'd had six mandulus attack him. As much as he didn't want to make a sound, his body betrayed him by releasing a groan like a punctured tyre leaking air. "Owwwwwwwww."

A cloudy view of his surroundings, Seb tried to raise his hand to wipe his face but couldn't. Heavy chains similar to the ones the net had been made from had been wrapped around him. Several blinks later, he saw they pinned him to an upright frame. A vertical rack of some sort. The realisation chased away the fog in his mind. They clearly weren't done with him yet.

It took several more blinks for Seb to fully realise his surroundings. An office of some sort. It looked cheap in its construction. With yellowing stud walls and the thick smell of salty damp, it had a desk in one corner that looked one strong shove away from collapse. Two chairs, both of them with torn upholstery and the browning foam hanging out of them like lolling tongues, sat to either side of it.

Just one window in the cheap space, Seb looked out into the warehouse beyond. Maybe the same one he'd been in when he was last conscious. Maybe he'd been out for long enough for them to take him somewhere else. Had they called Moses to come and collect?

"Nice to see you're finally with us."

Seb gasped as he jumped and turned to look in the direction of the speaker. The heavy chains rattled against the metal frame.

Unable to calm his rapid pulse, Seb breathed heavily as the lizard creature moved towards him. Even in the poorly lit office, its skin changed from green to blue as the light hit him from different angles.

A grin spread across his face, showing he had a mouth wide enough to catch a frisbee in. His gums were studded with small but sharp teeth, gaps between each one. But Seb saw them for the distraction they were and looked down at his captor's thick and powerful tail. It looked to be pure muscle and wore its barbs like a medieval club. One swipe of that thing would take his head clean off. Even at only five feet tall, it made sense why the mandulus called this creature boss.

A stale taste in his mouth, Seb gulped. As much as he tried, and as much as he hated himself for it, he couldn't hide the shake in his nervous voice. "What do you want with me?"

Before the lizard could respond, something moved in Seb's peripheral vision. Owsk stepped forward and Seb shook again. The chains rattled and the hard metal frame remained rigid. "You sold me out, you rat!"

A detached granite glare, Owsk watched Seb for a few seconds before he looked at the lizard.

As much as Seb wanted to continue to rip into Owsk, he

didn't matter at that moment. "Come on then," he said to the lizard, "whatever you have to do, get it done ... whatever your name is."

The lizard regarded Seb with its cold yellow eyes. A dark mind looked through that pallid stare, sending panic spiking through Seb. As often happened when he got backed into a corner, his mouth ran away with him. "That's how you want to be, is it? Go all dark and mysterious on me like the OG you are? If you won't give me your name, I'll have to give you one myself. I'll call you Buster."

A snap of its head to one side, an alien twist, the lizard creature said, "Huh?"

"Smuggler buster. That's what you do, isn't it? Bust being smugglers? Save the day by obtaining a commodity a grieving family would sell their soul for. And I thought drug dealers were bad."

A crocodilian smile, Buster shook his head. "You're quite a talker, aren't you?"

As he looked from Buster to Owsk and back again, Seb said, "Someone has to be."

A nod to concede the point. "So you've heard of me?"

"Only through that traitorous rat next to you." Both Seb and Owsk stared at one another again. Impossible to read the granite troll, Seb squirmed against the metal frame behind him. It proved as pointless as it had the first time.

"In that case, I'll forgive you for not understanding the gravity of your situation."

"You think you deserve more respect, do you?" A still-galloping pulse, Seb's mouth galloped faster. "I get out of trickier situations than this on a daily basis." It took until that moment for Seb to see the bloodstains in the concrete at his feet. Old bloodstains from where other beings had suffered the same fate that clearly awaited him.

When Seb looked back up again, he met a slight narrowing of Buster's yellow eyes. An agitated twitch sent his thick and powerful tail kicking out to one side. "You're not that smart, are you?" Buster said.

"I'm not the one hiring mandulus for protection."

"They dealt with *you* just fine."

"Your net dealt with me just fine. They simply stuck the boot in when I was down. A child could have knocked me out at that point."

Where irritation had tightened Buster's features, it seemed to fade away. "I don't know why, but I like you, Seb."

Seb didn't reply.

Buster shrugged. "So Owsk has told you a little bit about me, then?"

"For what it's worth, yeah. Although I'm not sure I trust much that comes out of that rat's mouth."

Owsk's deep inhale punctuated the quiet office's stagnant air.

"Well, I reunite families and take a small commission for saving their loved ones," Buster said, "just to cover my expenses. I also find the smugglers themselves. And when I do …"

"You drop them in the sea?" Seb said, unable to avoid looking at the dark stains in the concrete by his feet again. Even drowning seemed like a better prospect than the torture device he'd been chained to. Drowning would be over relatively quickly.

"The creature who's now at the bottom of the sea had a lucrative business in trafficking children," Buster said.

An involuntary wince twisted through Seb to hear that information, but he fought against it. As much as he wanted to believe what Buster had said to him, he couldn't take this creature at face value. He needed to remain objective until the lizard proved he wasn't a psychopath.

"Anyway, this isn't about him. This is about you. I must say, if Owsk hadn't vouched for you, I'm not sure we'd even be having this conversation now. You knocked out one of my guards. I'd like you to apologise to him."

The tall mandulu stepped from behind Seb. It had a swelling on its fat face.

When Seb twisted to try to look at the office space behind him—his chains rattling—he couldn't get far enough around to see. "Have you got any more of your crew hiding in the shadows?"

His hands clasped together in front of him, Buster repeated, "I'd like you to apologise to him."

"For him shoving a gun into the back of my head?"

"For knocking him out."

"Knocking mandulus out is like swatting flies. Something I'd do without much thought or effort. A bit like trampling daisies when walking through a field. How am I supposed to apologise for that?"

"Just apologise to him."

Seb looked back at the mandulu. "I'm sorry you're so easy to knock out. Even if you are a big lump."

"Is that it?" Buster said.

A sigh and Seb looked back at the mandulu again. "I'm sorry you have such a punchable face."

"My patience is wearing thin, Seb."

Unable to suppress his smile, Seb looked back at the mandulu and winked.

The beast tensed and straightened its back.

Seb's smile broadened. "Sorry."

Silence swept through the office again as they clearly waited for more from him.

The mandulu then looked at Buster. After a short and sharp nod from the lizard, the fat-jawed creature walked out of the office into the warehouse beyond. He slammed the door on his way out, the thin office wall shaking as a loud *crack* swept around the place.

"Bit temperamental," Seb said. "Having so many mandulus must make you feel like you're living with a group of teenagers."

Buster glared at him. "I've not known you long, but I feel like I understand you already."

The lizard's tone had changed. A little darker than before, it lifted panic into Seb's chest, tightening his lungs. As much as he'd stand toe to toe with the short reptile, in his current predicament, he had no chance. His shaky delivery under-mined his cocksure words. "How wonderful, a pop psychologist. You can never get enough of them."

"I think you're not very good at making friends."

"You just said Owsk vouched for me." Seb looked at Owsk. "Thanks for that, buddy. Although, you did lead me into this."

"I heard what you did to the *Piscents*," Buster said.

It even hurt to frown through the beating he'd taken, but Seb couldn't prevent it at that moment. "The what now?"

"My sub," Owsk said, his tone cold, his expression below freezing.

"Oh. Yeah. Well, I thought it was the right thing to do at the time. I wish I could take it back."

The emotion returned and Owsk raised his voice, his words echoing in the small office. "You keep doing what you think's the right thing. The problem is, you don't seem to think it through very well."

"Give me another example where that's true," Seb said.

"Um, I dunno … leaving your friends behind, maybe?"

After looking from Owsk and back to Seb a couple of times, Buster laughed. "So he does have friends, then? Don't get me wrong, there's something about his spirit I admire, much like I would a wilful child, but I find it hard to believe he'd have *actual* real-life friends."

"I know." Owsk shrugged. "Hard to believe, right? Although I would imagine his friends are a lot smarter than him." Then he turned back to Seb. "Maybe you should take their counsel from time to time. Maybe you wouldn't end up in so much shit."

The desire to get at Owsk tugged on Seb's sore frame, but even the slightest of movements met the resistance of the taut chains. Were he not bound to the metal rack, he would have swung for him by now despite vouching for Seb to keep him alive, and having helped get him away from Moses.

"Anyway"—Buster stepped between Seb and Owsk—"regardless of your clear hatred for one another, Owsk still vouched for you. He said, although you're an arsehole, you fly straight."

Seb shrugged and the chains rattled again. He looked at Owsk. "You have to understand that I didn't know what that sub meant to you." He then added in a softer tone, "I'm truly sorry."

Although Owsk looked like he wanted to reply, Buster lifted the dead grub up to Seb. "We took the liberty of removing this thing from your pocket. You want to find out where it's from, right? This is a part of your crusade to make the galaxy a better place?"

Seb nodded.

"Well, I can find out. And seeing as you're such a nice guy—that's sarcasm, by the way—I'll do it free of charge. Although understand this is a favour to Owsk, not you."

Seb held onto his snarky impulse and simply said, "Thank you."

"But I need a few hours."

"I haven't got a few hours."

"I hear you've upset the big man, so you're right, you really don't have a few hours. I'd imagine a bounty's already on your head. But, whether you have a few hours or not, I still need them to find out about this creature. If you can't wait, I can't help you." While holding the grub in Seb's direction, Buster said, "You're welcome to take it back and find someone else."

"You *know* I can't find anyone else."

Buster walked around the back of the robust frame and unlocked the chains holding Seb in place. The rush of heavy metal fell to the ground with a *whoosh,* gathering at Seb's feet like large metal snakes.

Once free of his bonds, Seb tried to roll some of the pain out of his sore body by twisting and turning.

Buster walked back around to stand in front of him. "So I'll see you in … let's say three hours?"

"It's not like I have a choice, is it?"

"We always have a choice. It's just sometimes the alternatives aren't very desirable. So see you back here in three hours?"

A slight shrug, Seb did his best to hide his petulance. "Fine." He didn't do a very good job of it.

CHAPTER 10

Neither Seb nor Owsk spoke as they stepped out of Buster's office into the warehouse beyond. Seb pulled the door closed behind him, the flimsy wood so thin it felt like cardboard.

A deep breath, Seb released some of his tension with a hard exhale. Thankfully he'd managed to walk out of Buster's office rather than leave the warehouse through the hole in the damp concrete ground. It might never have been the plan for him, but he'd had no way of knowing that at the time.

The large shutter remained up, the sun shining in through the huge space leading to the docks outside. Despite the bright glow, some corners of the warehouse remained impenetrably dark. Seb thought about the figure he'd seen when he'd been caught in the net. Lightning forks of pain ran through his face when he squinted to try to see better into the shadows. It made no difference. If they were there, he couldn't see them.

"I'm sorry," Seb said again, his voice echoing through the seemingly empty warehouse. "If I'd have known about the sub, I swear …" he trailed off. What more could he say about it?

Owsk didn't respond.

To get out of the warehouse, they had to pass the hole in the ground. Seb relived the moment when he'd seen the trafficker dropped into it. Not that he felt sorry for the creature, not if what Buster had said about it was true. Although, to look into the dark hole—the undulations of the sea running through the deep water—made his lungs tight and his breaths quicken. Because of his fists, he swam like a rock at the best of times, never mind being bound in heavy chains. Also, he had no SA to save him either.

"You know, you need to learn to stop being such a dick," Owsk finally said.

Seb bit back his initial reaction. At least they were talking. After a couple of seconds, he said, "I've had trouble with mouthing off before."

"Hmm," Owsk said.

"What does *hmm* mean?"

"And you haven't learned the lesson yet? You know Buster's OG, right? You joked about it, but he is. If he didn't owe me favours, then you'd be at the bottom of the sea like that rat he dropped in there earlier."

"It looked more like a hedgehog to me."

When Owsk shot him a glare, Seb pressed his lips tightly shut. A few seconds later, he added, "I hate to think what the seabed beneath this place looks like."

"Well, don't. Maybe think about what you can do to avoid being thrown down there with them."

"You could have told me what you were doing. I wanted to trust you, but when you led me into a welcoming party like that …"

Owsk tutted at Seb and shook his head. "You need to take

responsibility for your actions." Saltier than the air around them, the troll looked away, a craggy frown on his face.

The wind caught Seb off guard again when he stepped out of the warehouse. It crashed into him and threw him a couple of steps sideways, making the fabric of his trousers and top flap. Heavy with salt, the saline breeze had teeth that now chewed at the corners of Seb's eyes and mouth. As much as he wanted to rub them, it only made them worse. Besides, the bruising hurt too much to touch.

"I can't help it," Seb finally said, raising his voice over the howling wind.

Owsk kept up a brisk pace as he led them out of there, but he still turned to look at Seb as he walked. "Help what?"

"My reaction to tense situations. I know I turn into a dick. I should be dead by now a million times over. The thing is, when you can knock a creature out like I can, it makes you fearless."

"Stupid, more like."

The words stung, but Seb couldn't deny them. The taste of salt dried his throat when he swallowed. He then dipped a nod of concession at his granite friend. "Yeah, okay, stupid."

Owsk shook his head. "It doesn't matter how well you can fight when someone shoots a metal net at you."

Another nod. "I've found that out." The words stuck in Seb's throat as if his thirst clung onto them. "I'm sorry. *Again*. And thank you for vouching for me."

"I'm vouching for the prophecy. I believe in it."

The spaceport loaded with ships filled Seb's view. What would a few hours out there be like? Bad enough being human. But being human and being wanted by Moses …

Owsk stopped. Seb did too. The rock troll held a card in Seb's direction.

Black and plastic, the rectangle was no more than four inches wide and three inches tall.

Seb took it in a pinch and examined it. A plain black card. "What's this?"

"It's a travel card."

"Huh?"

"My family have been smugglers for centuries." After a deep breath as if to hold his emotions back, Owsk said, "As you know."

Seb nodded, the image of Owsk's sinking submarine running through his mind yet again.

"There's a network of smugglers who all have these cards. Show them to any ship's captain and they'll grant you free passage on their vessel."

"*Any* captain?"

"As long as they're not affiliated with any government or enforcement agency, yes."

Seb turned the black card over as if it would make something magically appear on it where it hadn't been before. "They don't look very hard to forge. How will the captain know to trust me?"

Owsk removed what looked like a small lamp from his pocket, flicked a switch on the side, and held it over the card. An emblem glowed on the black plastic. A circle with a submarine in the centre of it.

Neither Seb nor Owsk spoke as they both stared down at the card. The wind buffeted Seb's hair and clothes. He had to tense different parts of his body to fight against its push and shove. Owsk stood seemingly impervious to its effect, a rock in every sense.

When Owsk finally looked up at Seb, tears stood in his granite eyes. Although, when he spoke, his voice showed no hint of the emotion he clearly felt. "They'll know it's from me and that it's legit. They'll let you on their ship, no questions asked. You can be a ghost with this card and go wherever you need to."

"It seems like you've made a lot of friends and connections in your time," Seb said. Where he'd seen him as a small and meek character when he'd met him in the prison, he now saw him as so much more. Strength didn't always have to be worn like a badge of honour.

"I try my best," Owsk finally said. "Now get out of sight for a few hours. You'll need to go back to the warehouse on your own. I've got to get out of here. I've lost days being locked up in that damn cell. Days and hundreds of credits."

Seb opened his mouth to speak, but Owsk cut him off.

"Days, hundreds of credits, *and* a submarine."

Sadness sank through Seb's weary frame.

"Should you need any more help from me," Owsk said, "ask one of the captains to put a call out, and I'll come."

Before Owsk could say anything else, Seb stepped forward and hugged the creature. Despite his rough appearance, the strange-looking rock troll had a heart of gold. "Thank you."

Owsk didn't return the embrace, standing board stiff until Seb pulled away from him.

"Learn your lessons, Seb Zodo. This galaxy needs what you can bring to it. I just hope you have the presence of mind to work out what that is." And with that, Owsk turned his back on Seb and walked towards the spaceport.

The wind seemed to blow harder now that Seb found himself on his own. Harder and colder. Owsk had just shown him how it paid to make friends in this life. Not everything had to be a battle.

CHAPTER 11

Seb could have followed Owsk out into the spaceport to try to prolong their friendship, but he held back. Mainly because the rock troll had made it clear that their time together had come to an end. Not only had Seb sunk his legacy, but to associate with a human so publicly would be a black mark from virtually every other species. A human that maybe already had a bounty on his head. And if he didn't yet, he would soon. Besides, Seb had already asked too much of him, and Owsk had more than settled his debt for being broken out of the prison. Maybe their paths would cross again at some point.

The black card in his hand, Seb turned it over while he continued to stare at it. Owsk's emblem had glowed so brightly when he'd passed his lamp over it, but he couldn't see any trace of it now. To think of the submarine logo twisted another pang through his chest.

Still burning with the pain of the beating he'd taken from the pack of mandulus, Seb squinted against the wind as he looked over his shoulder at the warehouse. The salty onslaught continued to sting his eyes and forced his hair back. It rocked him where he stood.

Seb took the same route out of there that Owsk had about ten minutes previously. As he walked the pathway—flanked by two ships—he looked at each of the vessels. The one on his right loomed over him, casting the entire path in shadow. A flying warehouse, it must have made a fortune in freight if it filled its hull.

The ship on Seb's left must have been used for something other than smuggling. Small and aerodynamic, it clearly only carried passengers. Quite unusual on Aloo, as it seemed that most of the vessels there had a cargo of some sort. Why else would they come here? Maybe it was a satellite ship coming down from a larger fleet.

The second Seb stepped out into the walkway, the raucous commotion of a bustling spaceport crashed into him, hitting him harder than the wind had. A swirl of tens, if not hundreds, of conversations came at him from all angles. The collective funk of so many beasts and their meals forced him to crinkle his nose in disgust, aggravating the throbbing pain in his face. The thought of the sea slug he'd tried to eat the last time he'd visited turned his stomach.

It only took a few seconds before Seb could feel the attention of nearly every being on him. His world slipped into slow motion, but with such a large crowd around him, he had no chance of getting out of there if they turned on him.

A look to his left, Seb saw two brown, rocky creatures standing by their open ship. They both wore guns slung across their fronts, and they both held them like they'd use them in a heartbeat. Like they were desperate for the excuse, in fact. He dropped his attention to the ground.

A few steps later, Seb looked at the creatures on his right and met a similar hostility. Laser crossbows in their grips, the tall tree-like beings glowered at him. From left to right and everything in between, every being he looked at in the dense crowd seemed to be watching him.

As much as he tried to regulate his pulse with slow breaths, it did nothing, his heart hammering with such ferocity it threw him off stride. When he crashed into a large purple-skinned brute, it raised its top lip in a snarl at him.

After he'd walked no more than about twenty metres, both of Seb's shoulders hurt from where creature after creature had barged into him. To kick off now would start a fight he couldn't win. A fight the crowd seemed to want. He still couldn't tell if the hostility came from him being human, or if Moses had put the word out that he wanted him. A pain in his jaw from clenching it, he pushed on through the dense crowd.

At least Seb saw everything in slow motion. It made it much easier to navigate the hostile press of bodies, even if there were too many to avoid all the collisions. Biting his tongue as well as holding onto his physical desire to lash out, he looked up to see the next beast heading his way.

The creature wore a deep scowl and moved with a heavy gait. At least nine feet tall, it looked like a Sasquatch but red. Bright red. Hard to miss it in a crowd, especially when it strode directly at him. Anticipation sent the air around him electric, and Seb noticed some of the others watching the inevitable coming together.

As the monster drew close, Seb watched its entire large frame tense. It then twisted slightly, pulling its right shoulder back.

Its jaw clenched, its eyes narrowed, the crimson yeti scowled as it brought the right half of its body towards Seb.

Before it could connect with him, Seb jumped to the side. The air created by the red beast's swing pulled on his clothes as it whooshed past him.

Although Seb continued walking as if nothing had happened, he glanced over his shoulder in time to see the brute stumble into a family of hairy creatures with blasters. Even the children drew their weapons, the red creature raising its long arms defensively.

Seb dipped his head into the strong breeze and quickened his pace. Although he watched the ground, he threw the occasional glance around him. Shoulder barges were fine. Sure, they hurt, but he could deal with them. If it didn't escalate from there, he'd be okay. It also suggested he didn't have a bounty on his head. Surely something more would have happened by now if he did.

Another paranoid sweep of the area and Seb saw it. A shot of adrenaline forced a gasp from him. Through the crowd, in the shadow cast by one of the larger freighters, stood a figure. Maybe no different to many of the other figures around him—bipedal, similar proportions to a human, hell, it might even be a human—but he couldn't ignore the feeling he had when he looked at them. The same feeling that had followed him since he'd gotten out of Owsk's sub. The sense of someone sent by the Shadow Order to watch him. To bring him back to Moses. The crowd might not want him yet, but this creature certainly did. It had to be the same one he'd seen at the warehouse.

Ships still lined either side of the walkway, funnelling the sea breeze along it and casting the crowd in shadow. One of the largest vessels he'd seen had parked to Seb's right. A slow and subtle change of direction, he eased himself towards it. If he could get close enough, he could get under it and into the streets beyond before the silhouette twigged.

At first, the silhouette showed no sign of reading Seb's intention. He weaved and twisted to negotiate the crowded walkway, his heart rate lifting with the desire to run. The creatures around him still stared, but now he'd seen Moses' spy, they already seemed much less intimidating.

By the time Seb got close to the freighter, his body wound tight with his desire to get the hell out of there. He looked at the silhouette again. Something had changed in its form. It looked to have tensed slightly, like it had become more alert as it watched him.

He couldn't wait any longer. Seb shoved the first creature in front of him out of his way. The fat slug-like thing fell over from his push. The air around him lit up with indignation, cries of unrest and shock. Abuse aimed at his species.

Before they had a chance to lynch him, Seb burst free from the crowd and ran for the large freighter. When he looked behind, he saw the silhouette had given chase.

CHAPTER 12

The hairy little creatures guarding the large ship Seb ran at might have been small, but when they filed out of the ship's open cargo bay, they made up for in number what they lacked in size.

Little black eyes, they stared an intent at Seb that suggested they would destroy him—and he believed they felt that. Not that they'd be able to back it up in any way. Sure, they had sharp little teeth and attitudes that looked like they thought they could take over the galaxy, but it wasn't the first time he'd encountered diminutive creatures with illusions well beyond their abilities.

But Seb hadn't noticed the large block to the side of their cargo bay. Not until two of the creatures whipped the sheet away. He suddenly saw how they intended to back up their hostility. The confidence he'd felt only moments earlier drained from him, and he couldn't take his eyes from the large wheeled cannon they'd now revealed. "Damn," he muttered.

The small beasts worked as a team. Each no larger than a domestic cat, they moved as if all of them were connected to a hive mind. Four of them manoeuvred the base of the cannon to help aim it at Seb. Two of them jumped up onto the weapon and adjusted the barrel's trajectory. The two remaining critters stood on either side of the cannon. They held a pole between them, one on each end. To fire the weapon, it looked like they both needed to pull at the same time.

Even in slow motion they moved fast, but Seb kept running at them, the fat barrel of the cannon pointing straight at him. The screech of what must have been the lead critter gave him a warning.

"Halt, or we'll shoot."

When Seb looked over his shoulder, he saw the silhouette. Still unable to identify it, he could see it closing down on him. Halt and he'd get dragged back to Moses and the Shadow Order's base. Whoever chased him, if they came with Moses' backing, they'd be ready to take him down in whatever way they needed to. Be it a net made from chains or something similar, Moses would have made sure they were prepared to deal with Seb's abilities.

Already breathing heavily from the run, Seb pushed on as he charged at the critters. He shook his head at them but said nothing. No time for a debate.

The giant cannon had a barrel at least four feet long. It looked capable of issuing a laser blast large enough to vaporise his head. His steel-lined fists would do nothing against it. The two critters on top of it continued to make quick adjustments. Just metres separated them and Seb now. Slow motion helped, but he'd have to keep his wits to outsmart the tiny monsters.

A bright flash went off to Seb's right. It took his attention. Then a voice rang through his head. The loud instruction went off in his mind like a bomb.

"Down!"

So assertive, Seb followed it without thinking and dropped to the ground, rolling on the hard concrete. It reminded him of the kicking he'd only recently had from the mandulus, his face hurting the most, but the rest of his body still sore as it impacted the solid surface.

As Seb rolled over and over, he saw the cannon kick, throwing the two critters off the fat barrel. The blast started as a red streak and then spread to twenty times the width. A large and flat disc of light designed to cut something in two flew over him. The flash to his right had been done to distract him. The beam would have cleaved through him had the voice not shouted at him.

Seb rolled to a halt and watched the disc spin into the sky on an upwards trajectory. Although it would have taken him down, it travelled over the heads of those out in the spaceport and up into the sky. Then he saw the silhouette of his pursuer again.

Already aching from his day, Seb jumped back to his feet and ran at the critters and their cannon. The eight little creatures gawked at him as he passed, their tiny mouths forming perfect Os of shock. No time to fight back, Seb booted the one closest to him for good measure. It felt like kicking a deflated football, and he sent it spinning back into the hull of their large cargo ship. Hopefully it didn't kill it, but they needed to learn their lesson.

After he'd passed beneath the ship and burst out the other side, Seb looked at the line of shops in front of him. A dark alleyway ran between two of them. The entrance to a rat run of walkways, it had to be the best place to lose his tail. He just needed to maintain enough of a lead to keep the advantage. Gritted teeth, sweat pumping from him, and breathing hard, he dug deep and found a little more speed.

The thoughts of the voice in his head clouded his mind, but he shook them away. When he found safety, he could think about what had happened. Definitely not his own voice, but if he was losing the plot, he needed to deal with that once he'd gotten away from whatever chased him.

CHAPTER 13

The second Seb entered the alleyway, the slap of his footsteps bounced off the high walls and echoed away from him into the darkness. The noise made him an easy target to follow.

Upon rounding the first corner, dodging a couple of creatures that reminded him of large caterpillars, Seb saw a shop that looked familiar. Still at full tilt, his lungs tight, his feet slamming down against the hard ground, it took for him to watch it for a few seconds before it sank in. The shop Sparks had killed the electricity in. It almost made him smile. Were he not trying to get away from Moses' bounty hunter, his sore face contorting with the effort of his run, then he would have.

Several more twists and turns led to several more near collisions with beasts of every shape and size. Seb's legs ached to the point where he felt the strength draining from them. He couldn't keep this up indefinitely. The sound of his own struggle ran through him as he fought for breath. It prevented him from hearing whether he still had a pursuer or not. Safer to assume he did.

Just as Seb passed a kitchen on his left, a loud hiss burst

from an open window. He jumped away from it. Without breaking stride, he looked back to see a cloud of steam. It stopped him seeing the table laden with fruit and veg in front of him. When he clattered into it, the cheap wooden structure broke, sending him and all of the stock sprawling.

A monster of a creature with a horn in the centre of its face burst from the shop. Its features twisted into a contorted mess of fury. By the time it had opened its mouth to roar at him, Seb had already jumped to his feet and run off again. He called out, "Sorry," as if it would make a difference.

A moment to think when the alleyway straightened out, Seb's body wobbled from the demands he put on it. He had to do something other than run.

When he rounded the next bend, Seb stopped and rested against a cold wall. The wind from the sea barrelled through the tight walkways, blowing his hair back and cooling the sweat on his forehead.

Then Seb heard it.

Distant, but clearly the slap of his pursuer's feet. Impossible to tell and probably more a reflection of his exhaustion, but they sounded like they could run forever.

Seb's chest rose and fell with his heavy breaths. His heart beat so hard it felt like it would burst. He couldn't keep up this pace, but should he fight the creature? If it had been sent by Moses, it would be harder to beat than most.

A manhole cover sat nestled in the ground by Seb's feet. The sewers had been far from a pleasant experience the last time he went into them. Although, compared to the ones on Solsans, they were a stroll in a meadow.

The sound of his pursuer grew louder.

After another round of deep breaths to try to recover, Seb darted over to the metal circle and dragged it free. He bit down on his bottom lip as the large disc scraped over the concrete ground. A fine balance between removing it and not giving himself away.

The cover halfway clear of the hole gave Seb enough of a gap to squeeze through. The collective smell of a thousand creatures' excrement rushed up at him. It hit him on the back of his throat like two strong fingers and he gagged. Another look in the direction of his pursuer. Still no sign of them, but they sounded close. The last roll of the dice, he'd hide down below. If they followed him in there, he'd have to stand toe to toe with them.

Another quick scan around, Seb then slipped backwards into the sewers.

The temperature dropped as Seb descended. The metal ladder rungs were frigid and damp with condensation.

Once Seb had climbed low enough, the smells increasing with every inch he dropped down, he pulled the metal cover back in place. The same scraping noise as before: metal against concrete. Hopefully he'd done it quietly enough to keep his whereabouts hidden. The sewers were lit up. Only a weak glow, but enough to guide his way now he'd shut the light out above him.

At the bottom, the sound of rushing water louder than before, Seb waited and stared up. The back of his neck ached from looking straight up the ladder he'd descended, but he had to be sure he wasn't being followed before he moved on.

It only took a few seconds until the heavy stamps of something running over the manhole cover clattered above. Seb watched it, waiting for a spotlight as the cover was pulled back, but it never came. He heaved a relieved sigh. Maybe he'd gotten away.

A few hours to kill before he returned to Buster, Seb walked away from the ladders and delved deeper into the sewers. A walkway ran along the side of the river, the shitty water about a metre below.

The sewers in Aloo were similar to the ones in Solsans in many ways. But Aloo's sewers had lighting, albeit weak lighting. Dim bulbs sat encased in dirty glass domes every ten metres or so. It showed Moses understood the need for infrastructure and some level of investment. Even if that level could have been much higher. Better to build and maintain a sewer than risk an epidemic.

If Seb wanted to remain hidden, he'd have to tolerate the damp stench of shit and mould. But if it meant avoiding the Shadow Order's complex until he had answers, he'd stay down there for days.

Now Seb had stopped running, the aches and pains from the beating he'd taken in the docks, combined with the fatigue from his run, caught up with him. Were he to stop at that moment, he wouldn't move again, so he plodded on, his steps heavy, his legs leaden.

Seb's breaths finally levelled out as he rounded the next corner. Although the sewage ran a loud course in the canal, he heard something else and stopped. Just to be sure, he held his breath and listened again. Voices. High-pitched voices. Either children or tiny creatures. Either way, they sounded distressed.

Then it came back to him. So much had happened since he'd been down there last, what they'd experienced previously had slipped his mind. The being traffickers. Had they returned?

His back against the cold and damp wall, Seb slid along it and edged towards the sound. When he got close to the next bend, he stopped and listened to a voice close by.

"Shut up," it barked, its deep baritone booming through the sewer's tunnels.

Where the small voices had been just noises until that moment, Seb's heart twisted to hear one of them cry, "I want my mummy." It drew the breath from his lungs. It took all he had not to charge around the corner.

"You're dreaming if you think you're going back to her, boy." This time a gruff female voice.

Another female added, "You'd best get used to a life without her."

At least three beings around the corner, they all laughed. Their collective cackle sounded like sewage catching in a drain.

The sobs of what sounded like more than one child called through the sewers. The haunting call of loneliness. Of fear. Of losing hope.

When Seb peered around the corner, he saw a line of four small cages. Each one had two children in it. At least, they looked like children. The one that had spoken clearly was. Not many adults cried for their mummy, no matter how dire the situation. Three slavers stood in front of them, staring in at the wretched things. They all looked like they were the same species as the porcupine creature Buster had drowned. One of them raised a metal pole, stepped close to the sobbing child, stuck it through the bars, and jabbed it hard in the ribs.

The child yipped and withdrew to another round of cackling laughter.

Seb had only come down into the sewers to hide. To kill a few hours before Buster told him more about the parasite. He didn't need to get involved in this. It would save him a lot of hassle if he just walked away. Slavery happened. Everywhere. Jeopardising what he had to do wouldn't change that. Maybe he could tell Buster about it when he saw him. Yes, that would work. Buster sorted things like this out for a living. He'd know how to best deal with it.

Seb pulled away from the bend, turned his back on the traumatised children, and strode off in the other direction. Then he heard one of the slavers say, "Anyway, your mum's dead," and he stopped in his tracks.

The word that rang through his mind in the spaceport returned to him. *Down!* The female voice. The voice he didn't recognise. Or had maybe forgotten. It had been so long since he'd heard it. It had to be her. It had to be—

"Mummy," the child cried out again.

CHAPTER 14

Seb clenched his steel fists as he looked back at the bend he'd just peered around. A quickened pulse, he clamped his jaw and headed back towards the slavers and their victims. Who was he kidding? He couldn't walk away from this.

Unlike his last approach, Seb showed zero caution as he strode around the bend. He appeared in plain sight of the three creatures and caged children.

The child who'd called for its mum—a green frog creature—lay huddled in a ball. It whimpered but didn't call out anymore. A deep breath to slow his world down, Seb watched one of the other children point at him.

As one, the slaves and slavers looked at Seb.

A brief glance at the incarcerated children, Seb then shook his head as he took in the porcupine beasts. All three of the fat little things were brown and wore dirty sneers on their devious little faces. The tallest—if tall should even be used when considering the odd species—barely made it to four feet. It held the metal pole it had prodded the child with.

"There's nothing to see here," it said.

"That normally works, does it?" A nod past the creatures at the cages, Seb said, "Looks like there's plenty to see here."

The place looked like an underground plaza. The shitty water ran around the outside of the square of raised rock like a moat. Before the creature could reply to him, Seb strode directly towards it, closing down the few metres that separated them. Although he could have drawn his blaster, he kept it tucked into his belt. He hadn't come here to kill anything.

"Don't say we didn't warn you," the tall one said, brandishing its weapon. At that moment, all three of them doubled in size. Not that any of them grew taller. Instead, their flat spines popped out in every direction, turning them into deadly balls. The two that didn't have poles raised their fists to fight.

A look from one to the other, Seb couldn't see where to attack them. No weak spot stood out. If he punched them hard enough in the face, they'd probably go down, but he hadn't had this problem before. *Everything* had a weak spot.

The beasts rushed Seb. The lead one raised its pole above its head as if it were a sword. It yelled out with a feminine cry, and when it got close to him, it brought it crashing down.

Seb darted to the side, the pole sending out a splash of sparks as it connected with the concrete ground.

The creature who'd tried to attack Seb sprang backwards before dropping down into a defensive crouch. It left another one of the little beasts between them.

Seb lunged at the one closest to him and punched it in the face. It turned into a ball and rolled a few metres away from him before it got up again, apparently unhurt.

"Huh," Seb said to himself as he stared at the snarling thing.

The distraction gave the lead creature an opening. At the last minute, Seb saw the swinging pole and dodged it. The clang of metal connected with rock again. More sparks in the dark space.

Then Seb saw it. As he watched the pole-wielding brute retreat, he saw the weak spot in the centre of its back, buried deep within its spines.

The next beast came at Seb, the one he hadn't encountered yet. Although he knew it to be ineffective, he punched it in the face anyway. A crunch as his metal fist sank into its snout and it too rolled into a ball away from him. The other two rushed him again before he had time to think, the patter of their hard little feet crossing the cold ground between them.

This time Seb went on the offensive. He ran to the side to avoid the pole-wielder and punched the other one in the face again. He hit the thing so hard it lifted from the ground and flew backwards. Before it landed, it turned into a ball and rolled to safety. The punches must be hurting it, even if they didn't knock it out.

While the other two recovered, Seb looked at the leader's twisted face as it raised the pole again and attacked him. He avoided yet another skull-cracking blow, and as soon as the pole hit the ground for a third time, he brought a sharp chop down on the creature's left wrist.

A snapping of bone, Seb winced to watch the small beast's left hand fall limp as the pole clattered against the ground. It grabbed its injury while Seb grabbed the pole.

One of the other two came at Seb again. He lost track of which was which—not that it mattered. Both hands wrapped around the metal pole, he drove a full-bodied swing at it.

The end of the metal bar connected with the thing's small jaw. A wet crunching sound rang out and the creature spun away from him, turning back into a ball like they had every time he hit them. Although not as perfectly formed this time. It was clearly getting worn down from his attacks.

Seb chased after the rolling sphere of spines and jabbed his pole into the weak spot in the middle of its back. The creature unraveled instantly and ended up flat, its spines as flaccid as the rest of it.

Malice turned to fear in the eyes of the other two, but before they could react, Seb rushed forward. He came to the one with both wrists intact, whacked it with the pole, and then jabbed its weak spot as it spun around from his blow. The same limp reaction, it too lay on its back and stared at the ceiling.

The leader of the three had taken the opportunity to run, clutching its wrist as it moved. Seb gave chase.

The creature headed in the direction Seb had just come from. It vanished from sight momentarily as it rounded the bend.

When Seb followed it, he saw it running along the damp walkway next to the river. It moved fast for such a fat little thing.

The pole still in his hands, Seb gritted his teeth and sped up. The dim lights kept the creature in his line of sight. Then it disappeared around the next corner.

Seb panted as he ran to keep up with it. Whatever happened, he couldn't let it get up top. He'd only just lost his tail, he didn't need Moses locating him again.

Before Seb saw the creature, he heard its hard little feet against the metal rungs of the ladder. If he hadn't broken its wrist, it would be hard to catch. But when he got sight of it again, he saw it made slow progress.

The creature turned back and looked down at Seb. It bared a small mouth full of sharp teeth and hissed. Seb drove the end of the metal pole into its spiky back.

The beast fell and Seb could have caught it, especially as he saw its spikes droop. Instead, he stepped aside and let it hit the ground with an *oomph*. So loud, it sounded like it had driven all the air from its body. It lay motionless from being knocked out.

The creature's spines made a *whoosh* sound as Seb dragged it down the tunnel back to the slaves and its two unconscious friends. He then went to the first cage with the whimpering child in it and undid the lock. The frog creature looked up at him through watery green eyes, its lips buckling out of shape. It looked like it wanted to say something, opening and closing its distorted mouth, but no words came out.

Seb held his hand out to the small thing and helped it stand up. "I'm getting all of you out of here."

"And what about them?" Another prisoner—a tiny thing covered in blue fur—asked him.

"I'll lock them up down here. Give them a taste of what they gave you."

While Seb spoke to the small thing, he felt something on the back of his belt. By the time he'd spun around, he saw the frog boy with his blaster in his hand.

The kid aimed it straight at Seb, the weapon trembling with its grief.

"What are you doing?" Seb said.

Where he'd seen sadness in the kid's green eyes, he now saw fury. Rage shook the kid's entire form, but he said nothing.

CHAPTER 15

I t only took a few seconds for the kid to speak. It felt like longer to Seb as he looked between the end of the kid's shaking blaster and his watering eyes.

"Don't stop me," the boy finally said. The high pitch of his voice rang through the sewers, riding the sounds of the rushing water around them.

"It looks to me like you're the one calling the shots at the moment," Seb replied.

To Seb's relief, the boy turned the gun away from him. "What are you doing?"

The only response came in the form of three green blasts aimed at the unconscious slavers. Each one scored a direct hit, the porcupine creatures convulsing with the shots to the face.

Seb stared at the boy, the air hanging heavy with the stench of the slavers' singed hair and cauterised flesh. After a deep exhale, he said, "Damn."

What had been sad green eyes now steeled as they focused on Seb again. A shake of his head, the boy said,

"They *killed* my mum in front of me." Suddenly his fury broke and his body fell limp as if taken over with exhaustion. As he crashed down to his knees, he hunched over and addressed the damp, concrete ground, his voice wobbling with his grief. "And that wasn't the worst of what they did to us."

The other kids seemed to share in the boy's trauma. Not quite sure how he knew it, but Seb felt the collective sadness swell in the air around him. Whatever had happened, it had clearly happened to all of them. A shared experience that none of them seemed willing or able to talk about. Nausea balled in his stomach, forcing bile up into his throat.

If Seb had had the words at that moment, he would have used them. But how could he offer these children comfort? How could he begin to understand what they might have been through? The shock of the boy killing the slavers had gone. They deserved everything they got. In fact, a blast to the face seemed like a far too easy out for them.

It took until that moment for Seb to realise the kid still had the gun in his hand. He held his open palm in the boy's direction to take it back.

Although the kid reached across with it, just before Seb could close his grip around the weapon, the boy snapped the gun away from him, shoved the end of the barrel up against the bottom of his own chin, and pulled the trigger.

"Jeez," Seb yelped as he heard the wet pulse of laser fire and watched the blast fly out of the top of the kid's head, dragging brain matter and blood with it.

A cloud of crimson mist, some of it floated over to Seb and rested against his face. He kept his lips tightly pressed together while he wiped it away with a shaking hand.

Then the first child cried. A second later a couple more

started up. It took just a few moments for every one of them to break down. Seb used all his strength to stop himself from crying with them. He swallowed against the rock of grief wedged in his throat and looked down at the froggy kid. He lay face down. Limp. Lifeless.

CHAPTER 16

A small time passed as Seb stared at the dead child. The damp weight of sadness dragged on his heart and rooted him to the spot. It took for a little hand to slip into his to break him out of it. When he looked down, he saw the tiny kid with the blue fur. Damp tracks ran down her hairy face and her eyes searched his. She needed an adult's guidance. They all did. For the first time since he'd been in Aloo, it didn't matter about him being human, the only thing they cared for was his help. He pulled his shoulders back and straightened his posture before nodding at the little girl. Together they turned to the cages behind them.

Once Seb had freed all the children—the newly liberated slaves helping as they moved down the line of cages—he turned back to the slavers and the dead green boy. As much as he wanted to speak, the threat of tears wouldn't let him. The sound of rushing water ran through the cavernous space. The drips of leaks were everywhere. The heavy breaths of the scared and grieving children.

For the act of it if nothing else, Seb walked over to the largest of the three porcupine creatures, the one he'd broken the wrist of. He grabbed its ankles and dragged it towards the edge of the stone platform they were currently on.

To look down into the churning mess of waste flipped Seb's stomach. The brown river turned over on itself as it rushed through the sewers. A thick and rancid mix of toxins and disease. He looked from it to the lead slaver and then to the dead boy. All of the other children had gathered around the kid's corpse. They all looked at Seb.

A clenching of his jaw, Seb then screamed through his gritted teeth and kicked the vile beast in the back.

The sound of his blow echoed through the tunnels as a slap. The creature rolled in midair as it fell from the ledge and plummeted into the river below. It hit the water with an unceremonious splash before vanishing beneath the surface. No doubt it would wash up on Aloo's shores at some point in the next few days. Not that a dead body in Aloo would surprise anyone. Hopefully such a frequent occurrence, no one would bother to investigate, but even if they did, they had no way of tracing it back to him.

Just as Seb thought to go back for the other two slavers, he saw the children bringing them to him. They sent them the way of their leader.

A line of seven little beings from all over the galaxy, they stared down into the river and watched the space where the creatures had vanished beneath the surface. They needed that.

When one of the children walked over to the frog boy and grabbed his ankles, Seb shook his head. "No," he said. His voice cracked when he added, "He's not going in *there*."

"Then where?" the child, a hairless bipedal cat, said.

A good question. They could hardly find somewhere to bury him. "We need to leave him down here," Seb said.

Confusion stared up at him.

"Hardly ideal, I know, but we can't take him above

ground. Not if we want to get you lot out of here without any drama." Did he believe that? Most beings, no matter how ruthless, would want to help the children. But if he had a tail sent to follow him by Moses, he didn't need to be coming above ground and making a fuss with the body of a dead child. It wouldn't bring the kid back to life. "I don't think he should be dumped in the water. He deserves more than we just gave those *things*."

Before Seb could say anything else, all of the remaining children gathered around the frog boy. They went to work on him, straightening his clothes and crossing his arms over his chest.

It only took a few seconds before they stepped away from his corpse. Seb's eyes itched and his world blurred. The kid lay on the damp stone ground. His green eyes were glazed with his passing, but he looked at peace, a halo of blood pooling around his head. The torment of only a few minutes ago had left him; forced through the top of his skull by a green laser blast. As sad as his suicide was, it made sense. Just a shame he couldn't see any other way to process what had happened to him.

Seb walked over to the boy and crouched down next to him. He stared into his dead face and stroked his brow. "Be at peace. Find your mum, kid." The gods knew he'd thought about ending it all himself. A thousand times at least. When his time came, he'd get to see his guardian angel again. She probably looked down on him now. The call of *down* rang through his memory. Maybe not a strange voice. Maybe just a voice he hadn't heard in a long time.

When Seb looked back at the children, he met the stares from seven small and dirty faces. Although he cleared his throat, it did little to banish the emotion in his voice. A warble ran through his words. "I know we're not exactly in the nicest of places," he said, "but we need to wait it out in the sewers for a few more hours. After that, I'm going to take you to someone who can help you. But I don't want to wait in this exact spot. We can all say goodbye to …"

"Artez," the blue-furred girl said.

Seb nodded. "Artez. We can all say goodbye to him; then we need to find somewhere else."

The kids formed an orderly queue, the blue-furred girl at the front. Seb watched them say goodbye to Artez one by one.

CHAPTER 17

A large creature similar to the brown hairy one in the prison cell—the one that looked like Bruke—walked into Seb. The impact sent fire through his right shoulder and spun him almost all the way around. Instinct took over. He clenched his metal fists, slowed his world down, and glared at the brute. It stared straight back, more than ready for the fight it didn't realise it had no chance of winning.

But Seb turned away from the creature and continued on, moving through the bustling crowd in the busy spaceport. The only human from what he could see, he pushed forward and took the knocks. Let them try to intimidate him; it didn't matter. It still seemed like the resentment came because of *what* he was rather than *who* he was. He could only assume Moses hadn't put the call out for him yet.

What sounded like a million different accents filled the air in the spaceport as creatures shouted at one another. So many voices, the sound turned into white noise for all but the ones closest to Seb. The creatures farther away could be talking about him. Hard to imagine they wouldn't be with how they all stared at him. But he couldn't kick off, especially not now.

The few hours in the sewer had helped Seb lose his tail. At least, he'd seen no sign of it yet. For all the attention on him at that moment, he couldn't feel the watchful eye of someone specifically sent to track him down. Although, like a salamander, he might have lost one tail, but he'd grown another.

A look over his shoulders on both sides and he ran through the count. One, two, three, four, five, six … His heart sped. Six?! Seb stopped and the six stopped too. They were to follow him, stay in sight, but not get too close. A human in the spaceport attracted enough attention. If he had seven slave children with him, he wouldn't last two seconds without something kicking off. Then he saw her, the small blue hairy one. He'd not asked their names because he didn't want to get too attached. A relieved sigh, he set off again.

To walk between the two ships on either side of the alleyway to the docks made the guards on the cargo bays of each ship bristle. On his left he saw four beasts. They held chrome handles that would no doubt produce a laser sword of some description. Two guards on the other side, they went for the more traditional semi-automatic blasters. Both crews utterly different from one another were united in what appeared to be a desire to obliterate humanity.

Although he had to remain vigilant to the threat, they really didn't matter at that moment. Seb stared straight ahead as he headed towards the docks. The children followed him.

The wind on the other side of the ships ran across the expanse of open concrete straight into Seb. All of Aloo stank of salt, but having it rammed in his face intensified the stench.

Where he'd lost the small blue hairy creature in the busy spaceport, Seb saw her come through the walkway first. He tapped her on the head as she passed him. "One."

Several more came through behind her. "Two, three, four, five."

A look up the alleyway and Seb saw six and seven walking towards him. But then one of the creatures from one of the cargo ships stepped in front of them. One of the ones with the swords.

"Wait there," Seb said to the five children and he headed back up the walkway. "What's the problem?"

The creature with the sword didn't look capable of wielding it. Fat, flabby arms, tyres of blubber running around its middle. It looked at Seb and lifted its plump top lip in a sneer. "What are you doing with these kids?"

"Taking them to someone who can help them. They were slaves."

"You bought them?"

Seb dropped his voice to a low growl. "I *rescued* them."

"They're valuable."

The two remaining children were mandulus. They were even ugly as kids, but they were kids nonetheless. They were so young they still had their horns. Seb moved between them and the fat swordsman. He shoved both of them in the direction of the others and said, "Go and be with your friends. I'll catch up."

"I can't let you do that," the creature with the sword said. A quiet click and the metal handle of the sword produced a purple, cutlass-shaped blade.

The fighting grew tiresome, but sometimes it resolved things quicker than anything else could. In one swift movement, Seb shoved the creature back, its skin slimy as if it secreted sludge. Before it had time to think, he punched it in the centre of its fat head.

The swordsman hit the ground hard and the two kids ran to be with the others. Seb leaned down and pulled its sword from its unconscious hand. When he cut the weapon through the air, it felt sharp enough to slice through the salt on the wind.

The blade still in his hand, Seb turned to look back at the creatures guarding either ship. First he looked at the sword wielder's friends, and then he looked at the two beasts with the semi-automatic rifles. He raised his eyebrows at each group, inviting them to step forwards.

None of them took the offer.

While pointing the purple blade down at the unconscious beast, Seb said, "I don't know what he thought to do with those children, but they're going to be reunited with their families. When he comes to, make sure he knows I spared his head. But if he even thinks about trafficking, *especially* children, I'll be back for it."

Other than the wind, Seb heard nothing, so he looked at the unconscious beast's friends. "Okay?"

The creatures nodded.

Then to the two with blasters. "That goes for you too."

They also nodded.

The sword's handle had a small button on the grip. Seb pressed it and the blade vanished. He then slipped the weapon into his pocket.

Seb walked towards the docks, stepping out of the alleyway into the harsh wind again. The skin around his lips and eyes stung worse than ever. The sooner he got away from Aloo, the better.

CHAPTER 18

"One, two, three, four, five, six, seven," Seb said as he did another head count and set off again. Now they had an expanse of concrete between them and the chain-link fence sectioning off Buster's warehouse; hopefully none of them would go astray.

Where Seb had struggled against the battering from the wind, he glanced behind to see the children had lined up in single file behind him. And he couldn't begrudge them using him as a barrier against the elements. The assault ran so hard into him, it would probably lift the kids off their feet if they tried to brave it on their own.

Only a fifty-metre walk at the most, but by the time Seb reached the gate in the chain-link fence, the skin on his face had pulled so taut it felt like it could crack.

A nine-foot-tall mandulu with a swollen face appeared when they got closer. It wore a blaster on a thong across its chest, just like it had the last time Seb saw it. It glared harder at him than before, almost as if it had been plotting its revenge for the beating he'd given it.

The creature looked like it wouldn't say anything, so Seb shrugged. "Buster said to come back in three hours."

The mandulu paused for a few seconds, its chest rising and falling with its heavy breaths. "You're early."

Seb shrugged again. Ten minutes early at the most, he didn't reply because he couldn't be bothered with the argument.

A snort of air from its fat snout, the mandulu waited for a good minute before finally opening the gate, letting Seb and the little ones in.

Just before Seb rounded the corner to enter the warehouse, he stopped and raised a halting hand at the kids. Seven small faces looked up at him. "You need to wait here while I go and see Buster. I need to warn him what's about to enter his life before he sees it." A look at the mandulu on the gate, he saw it still staring back at him. Although it hated him, he could see it wouldn't harm the kids. As one of Buster's guards, it probably knew how to handle them much better than Seb did.

Seb looked back at the children. None of them spoke. Hopefully all seven would remain where they were.

When he entered the warehouse, Seb flinched at the sight. Good job he hadn't brought the children with him. A scene similar to the one he'd encountered the first time he'd visited —Buster, six mandulus, and one shady-looking character wrapped in chains all stood over the hole in the warehouse's ground.

Buster looked up at Seb, flashed him a reptilian smile— his eyes cold, his teeth wonky—and then he pushed the chained creature into the water with a splash. He wiped his hands, his laugh ringing out through the warehouse. "I should have a new tag line for my business: *Cleaning up the galaxy one slaver at a time.* Maybe I'll get some stationery made up, what do you think?"

Seb nodded at the pit the slaver had just been dropped into. "You might have to make a new hole. Many more bodies in that one and the pile of corpses will reach the surface."

The same crooked smile remained before Buster said, "You're early."

Owsk had seemed like a stand-up kind of being. He wouldn't trust Buster if he couldn't be trusted. But now Seb had to hand children over to the creature, he had to question the decision. What would he do with them? What if he couldn't get them back to their parents? But what else could he do? Not like he could take them with him. And Owsk trusted him. "I found a bunch of slaves while I was out."

Buster's frame sank and his wonky smile fell.

"Seven of them. Children." If only it were eight. Seb pulled in a deep breath to settle his emotions.

A tilt of his head to one side, but Buster still didn't reply.

"I couldn't leave them."

This time Buster looked past Seb at the entrance of the warehouse. "Where are they?"

"Kids," Seb called out and clapped his hands to get their attention.

The small blue hairy one led the way. A line of tiny beings with wide and fearful eyes followed her. Even Buster softened at their appearance.

It took a few seconds before Buster looked away again and called to one of the mandulus. "Take them into holding. Feed them, get them washed up, and find out where the hell they're all from. We need to get them back home."

"Think of the fees," Seb said with a shrug. "It's all cred-its, right?"

Buster cocked an eyebrow at him and spoke with a slow and cold voice. "Right."

Although Buster didn't invite him, when he walked towards his decrepit office, Seb followed.

The second Seb entered the room, he looked at the metal frame he'd been tied to. A once white, now yellowed, sheet had been draped over it, hiding both it and the bloodstained floor surrounding it. Should he really be handing over vulnerable children to this creature?

After Seb had closed the door behind himself, he opened his mouth to speak. But before he could get his words out, something knocked from outside.

"Come in," Buster yelled.

The face of a tall and skinny red creature poked its head into the room. Its eyes were the colour of cocoa and sat on opposite sides of its blade-shaped head. It looked like it belonged in the sea. It stared at Seb and Seb stared back.

The creature entered the room and closed the door behind it. To see it in its tall and skinny glory showed just how impoverished it was. No meat on its bones, its clothes were filthy and torn to shreds. It gripped an envelope in its long hands, the cream paper as mucky as everything else to do with it.

The smell of dirt walked past Seb with the creature. It stopped in front of Buster. "I've come to deliver the first payment for returning Alicia to us. Thank you again, sir, we're forever in your debt."

Although Buster wore a permanent scowl, which he levelled on the wretched thing in front of him, he said, "Keep it."

Both Buster's tone and demeanour suggested hostility, so it took Seb a few seconds before he said, "Huh?"

An awkward silence followed as the other two stared at

Seb. The red being then turned back to Buster. "I don't understand."

"Keep it. You need the credits. I can't take them from you. Tell you what, I'll make you a deal. If you ever come into a fortune, remember your debt. Otherwise, forget about it. I've just wiped your slate clean."

The red creature didn't reply, its long mouth falling open as it twisted its grip around the envelope.

"Oh, one more thing," Buster said.

It had seemed too good to be true. Seb's stomach twisted in anticipation of Buster's imminent act of cruelty.

"Don't tell *anyone* I've not made you pay. I don't want the galaxy and their neighbours thinking I'm a soft touch. I have to make a living, after all." Before the creature could respond, Buster pointed at it. "If I find out that you've told anyone, I'll expect every penny of the fee, okay?"

The red creature looked no less scared of Buster now than when he'd entered. While bending over as if halfway through a bow, he backed out of the room, repeating the words, "Thank you."

When the door closed, Seb looked at it for a second. He then looked at Buster, who scowled at him. No wonder his office looked like crap. If he never collected, he probably didn't have the credits he should in his line of work.

What small break there had been in Buster's saltiness returned and he damn near spat his words at Seb. "I only charge those who can afford it." He sighed. "Unfortunately, so few beings can afford it." The scowl returned. "Let's hope one of those little brats you brought to me has a rich mummy and daddy; otherwise I'll be coming to *you* for the fees."

Any doubt Seb had had about bringing the kids to Buster suddenly vanished. They'd all get to where they needed to go. "So how did you get on with the parasite I brought to you?"

While glancing at his nails, Buster shrugged. "I need longer."

"What do you mean?"

"It's pretty simple, isn't it? I need longer." Although Seb opened his mouth to reply, Buster said, "The parasite has been genetically manufactured."

"And?"

He fixed Seb with a yellow glare. "What that means is it comes from a lab. Therefore, it's much harder to trace who both made and then, subsequently, who bought it. It could have come from one of many farms that create that kind of crap. On top of that, I have to find a way to get access to their confidential files on who purchased it. When they sell a species to someone, they don't want that thing being tracked back to them or the purchasers. Their clients could be using the creatures for organic weapons."

"Which nine times out of ten, they probably are," Seb said. "So you won't be able to trace it?"

"I didn't say that. Just that I need longer." Buster pulled open one of his desk drawers and fished out a satellite phone. "Here," he said as he held it in Seb's direction.

Seb took the large device and looked at it for a few seconds. So large he couldn't wrap his hand all the way around it. It looked old, like most of Buster's equipment. "I've seen bricks smaller than this."

A raised eyebrow, Buster said, "I'll call you when I have more information. Just keep your head down so Moses doesn't find you."

"What do you know about Moses?"

"This is Aloo. Moses runs the place. I know he's just put out the word that he wants you. Dead or alive. I'm not sure it's public knowledge *yet*, but it will be soon. I know he's not someone to be crossed. I know he'll shut me down, wrap me in chains, and throw me into the sea if he hears I'm helping you."

"Yet you still want to help me?"

Another shrug, Buster stared at his nails again, faking nonchalance. "I know what Moses is like. If you have reason to believe someone has wiped out a colony with the parasite and that he's gaining from it, I'm inclined to believe you. From what I've seen, the world would be a better place with that shark gone."

"So how long do I have to lie low for?"

"Three to five days. Maybe a week."

"A *week?* I won't last a week on Aloo."

"The information isn't going to be easy to find."

Although Seb wanted to argue, what could he say? Buster had gone well beyond the favour he owed Owsk. "Where do you suggest I go?"

"Not my problem."

"I'm not saying it is. I was just looking for some advice."

"The sewers are always a good place to hide."

The suggestion deflated Seb. No way could he spend three days down there. And if it took a week … "Okay," he finally said. "Thank you for everything you've done for me. I'll be waiting for your call."

Buster had stared at his nails for most of the conversation. When he looked up, the slightest crack of compassion lifted his stony face. "Good luck, Seb. Stay safe and stay hidden."

Seb nodded and walked out of his office. Remaining safe and remaining hidden were easier said than done for a human on Aloo. Especially a human wanted by Moses.

CHAPTER 19

No better existence than a rat, Seb sat in the darkness of Aloo's sewers, hunched over and motionless save for his slow breaths. The festering stink around him had permeated his psyche and had delved deep into his aching joints. He hadn't moved for hours and didn't plan on it any time soon.

At least three days. Three days to a week according to Buster. Maybe it wouldn't be so bad. Who was Seb kidding? It would be awful. But could he tolerate it?

Once he'd climbed down into the sewers, Seb had found an underground plaza like the ones used by the slavers. That was where he chose to wait, sitting on the cold and damp ground. He hadn't moved since. The muggy air had left a layer of moisture on his face. Unlike the blood mist, he didn't bother to wipe it off.

With one liberated laser sword in his pocket and his blaster stuffed down the back of his trousers, Seb held onto the brick of a phone Buster had given him. For at least two of the three hours he'd been down there for, he stared at the device, willing it to ring.

Seb had zero desire to move. A good job, because he

might not have heard the sound otherwise. Even without his own motion, the roar of rushing water and loud drips from leaky pipes almost hid it. Almost. But when he heard the tock of a foot against one of the many ladder rungs, he gasped. The sound of his surprise rushed away from him into the darkness. Had he just given up his advantage?

When Seb stood up, he wanted to groan from the effort, but he kept it in this time. His muscles already hurt before he'd climbed down into the damp underworld. Too much action and not enough rest. Thanks to his time in the sewers, his joints now ached too. The heavy, chilly air ran into the cartilage in his hips, his elbows, his knees …

Seb did his best to tune out the sound of the rushing river of shit. The loudest noise down there by far. He strained his ears and heard it again. *Tock.* It hadn't been his imagination. Foot against metal. Something was coming down into the sewers, and they were close.

In his present location in the relative open of the sewers, Seb would be found straight away. More appealing than the dark walkways in the tunnels, but an awful place if he wanted to remain unseen. They'd take him back to Moses and he'd never learn where the parasites came from.

After Seb had pushed himself to his feet and taken a few laboured steps, he loosened up a little and found his stride. The width of the rivers of shit were consistently large. Too large to leap across except for in the open spaces like the one he was currently in. In each corner, the gap tightened, so he ran for one, jumped over to the walkway on the other side, and vanished around a dark corner in the opposite direction from the sound.

As much as Seb would have liked to make a stealthy escape, the slap of his feet against the damp ground called through the underground network of tunnels. Another noise for his stalker to follow.

Because he'd relinquished his chance to be quiet, Seb gave up the pretence and sped up.

Seb heard his pursuer do the same, the slap of feet chasing after him.

A faceless foe—fast and closing down on him—threatened to rob Seb of his resolve. In his mind, he saw a monster with a large mouth and sharp fangs. A minotaur in Aloo's labyrinthine underground tunnels.

The weak lights did little to show Seb the way. He saw the right-angled left turn too late. Although he tried to take it, the damp ground didn't give him the grip he needed. His feet slipped from beneath him. His world shifted into slow motion as he slammed down on the wet concrete. The impact jabbed a hot poker into his left hip. It balled in his stomach as a need to vomit.

Unable to control his pain, Seb rolled on the ground, cradling where he'd hurt himself. His legs hung out over the river, but not far enough for there to be a chance of him falling in.

The light pad of feet on Seb's tail pulled him from his agony. He pressed his hand against the cold and damp wall to make it easier to stand up. The pain in his hip ratcheted up when he put pressure on it, but he had to keep going. A clenched jaw and heavy breaths, he pushed through it and took off again into the darkness. No way would he be beaten down here. Moses didn't deserve the satisfaction.

More alert after his fall, Seb saw the next bend this time and sailed around it. He moved with a limp, and the steps behind him were clearly getting closer. Then he found a ladder.

The same damp and rusty rungs he'd seen on every other ladder, Seb grabbed on and pulled himself up.

The sound of his own feet against the metal paled in comparison to the running footsteps closing in on him. To climb hurt his hip more than running. His heart hammered. His lungs tightened. Sweat turned his palms damp. But he kept going.

At the top of the ladder—the footsteps closer than ever—Seb reached up and shoved the manhole cover aside. Metal scraped over concrete, ringing out for his pursuer to hear.

Despite it being the middle of the day, the tight alleyway was dark with shadow, although not as dark as the sewers. Seb dragged himself out of the hole and fell onto the hard concrete ground. He then twisted around and slid the manhole cover back across, panting and shaking with exhaustion.

Not only had the manhole cover been made from steel, but a metal ring had been implanted in the ground so it fitted back in perfectly. Seb clenched his fist as he stared at it, got up onto his knees, and yelled as he drove a punch against the edge of the hole. It bent the steel ring surrounding the cover, pushing it slightly over the protective disc. Another punch on the opposite side yielded the same result. Two more punches left it with a distortion on each compass point.

When Seb tried to pull the manhole cover free, he couldn't. It would slow his pursuer down at the very least.

Seb groaned again as he moved off. His body didn't feel ready for it, but he needed to get out of there. He might have bought himself some time, but he didn't know how much.

The alleyways were quiet, but not abandoned. As Seb ran away from the manhole cover, he passed the watchful glare of an old female tisk. She stared at him through cataract eyes. And why wouldn't she? Being human on Aloo was enough of a curse. A human with a wicked limp, ragged breaths, gushing sweat, and no doubt stinking of excrement was a veritable beacon. It wouldn't be long before Moses found him. He couldn't last on Aloo for three days, let alone a week. He had to get out of there and find somewhere safe to wait for the phone call. The next time he came back would be to find out about the part Moses had played in killing Wilson's family. Then he'd gladly let himself be taken to the shark-faced crook.

CHAPTER 20

Far enough away from the sewers and no sign of his pursuer, Seb rested against a wall as he caught his breath. Not yet in the spaceport, he watched the occasional creature pass him and they stared back. Whether they'd heard about the bounty or not, he still couldn't tell.

You need to look after yourself.

"Who's that?" Two ape-like creatures looked over at his outburst. He glared at them and replied in his head. *Who are you?*

Just look after yourself, Seb. You need to get off Aloo.

I know that, Seb replied. *But where shall I go?*

The voice didn't respond. It didn't need to. He knew where he had to go. He'd known it all along. And now he'd run out of options, he couldn't ignore it any longer.

CHAPTER 21

As a human on Aloo, Seb might as well have worn a flashing target on his back. Every time he sneezed, the entire planet turned to stare at him. Hell, every time he breathed, something seemed to be displeased with his presence. Or so it felt. But even as he moved into the more populated areas of the cursed planet, he'd still not seen any sign that the creatures around him wanted to claim the bounty Moses had put on his capture. Maybe it still hadn't become common knowledge.

On his way back to the spaceport, Seb came to a row of four shops, all of them as ramshackle and disorganised as the next. He paced up and down outside them a couple of times, looking at the shopkeepers through their cluttered windows. For no other reason than the beast behind the counter looked the least hostile—on account of being the smallest of the lot —he shrugged and walked in to the left one of the four.

A bell above the door let out a weary ring when Seb opened it, and the shopkeeper looked up at him as he entered. What had been close to a hospitable expression on the small orange creature's face darkened and turned into open displeasure. "Oh," it said.

If the small beast had that reaction to him, what would the larger ones have been like had he chosen their shops? Before Seb had time to think on it any further, the strange little thing —no larger than a domestic cat and nowhere near as pleasing to the eye—produced a cannon of a blaster. Three times larger than its wielder at least, the barrel of the gun looked big enough to slide Sparks into. The weapon looked capable of turning a freighter to dust.

"Easy now," Seb said, his hands raised defensively. "I'm not here to make trouble."

"What are you here for, then?" the small orange being barked.

Seb looked around the cluttered space. Shelves everywhere, mostly laden with tat, he couldn't see what he wanted. "A cloak?"

"And what if I don't have one?"

Hard not to look at the large weapon trained on him, Seb swallowed against his rapidly drying throat. The dust in the air then ran up his nostrils and he scrunched his nose against the tickle of it. He'd still not spoken because his mouth had gotten him into too much trouble in the past. He needed to keep his head. "If you don't have one," he finally said, "I'll say thank you for your time and go next door."

Only slightly, but the end of the creature's blaster sagged in reaction to Seb's comment. It didn't reply.

Unsure what to do with the silence, Seb shrugged and tried to keep his agitation from his tone. "Should I go?"

A dark scowl, the beast said, "What kind of cloak?"

"One that hides my face."

"Not surprised."

Indignation snapped Seb tense. "I'll be going next door, then, shall I? I came in here because you looked like the *least* aggressive of all the shopkeepers."

"Bad choice." A shake of its head, the creature sneered. "Hate humans."

It almost made Seb laugh. At least it spoke its mind. He shrugged. "You and everything else on this stinking planet."

"Especially ones that have upset Moses."

A cold rock of dread plummeted through Seb and he pulled in another deep breath. The sides of his vision blurred as his gift threatened to kick in. A tense situation, it had suddenly turned potentially volatile. To stop his sass spilling out of him, he thought about every word before he spoke them. "Look, can you give me a cloak or not? I've not come here to discuss your prejudices. In fact, I couldn't care less about them."

"And Moses?" the creature said.

Seb stared at it. What little ground he'd made with it lowering its blaster, he lost as the vicious little beast raised its weapon again. Step one, get a cloak. Deal with that first.

After another few seconds of staring at one another, Seb said, "I'm going to leave now. I've not got all day."

"Wait," the creature said, the anger in its voice losing out to desperation. It needed credits and Seb needed a cloak.

The creature put its gun down on the counter. "Got cloak. Would fit you. Finest fur. Shame to use it on human. Such a waste. But you can have it."

"A human's credits still work, you know? I'll give you one hundred for it."

"Two hundred."

Seb laughed. "One fifty, and you forget you ever saw me, okay?"

The beast glowered at Seb for a few more seconds before it accepted his offer with a nod of resignation. "Moses is offering a lot more, you know."

For the first time since he'd walked in, Seb shot a reactive response back at him. "You and I both know you don't want the fight."

The creature stared at him for a moment as if it would challenge him. It looked down at its blaster. The silence seemed to last forever before it nodded. "You're right. I hate humans, but I don't think much of that shark either."

After the transaction, Seb threw the cloak over himself. It wasn't made from fur like the scheming little beast had suggested. It felt more like a cheap sack woven from coarse brown string. "A cloak fit for a monk," he said. It did, however, hide his face and masked the smell of the sewers. It also had pockets he could put his blaster, laser sword, and satellite phone in. Maybe dressing as humbly as he could would see him in good stead. The less attention on him, the better.

Step one complete, Seb looked at the vulgar little crea-ture. In a flash, he pulled the beast's cannon out of its reach and said, "If Moses finds out I've been here, I'm going to come into your shop while you're sleeping and burn it to the ground with you in it. You got that?"

What had been a seriously bad attitude yielded to fear. The creature's hard frown softened and it looked at Seb for a few seconds. "I told you I don't like him."

"Have you got that?" Seb repeated, raising the cannon.

A reluctant nod, but a nod nonetheless.

Seb slid the gun back across the counter to it. "Good." He then spun on his heel and left the shop. Not easy to trust the creature, but it didn't change anything. He had to find a ship and get off Aloo as soon as he possibly could. The sooner the better, so when Moses did find out, which he inevitably would, he'd be long gone.

CHAPTER 22

Whether the shopkeeper had ratted him out or not, Seb didn't have long left on Aloo. If the shopkeeper didn't tell Moses, enough creatures had seen him that one of them would. If Moses wanted him as much as he expected he did, the Shadow Order shark would shut the port down if he got a confirmation of him still being there.

A check of his reflection as he passed a window, Seb saw that the cloak completely covered his face. The brown, ratty fabric restricted his view, but the limited visibility was a small price to pay to remain hidden.

Now he'd made the decision to leave Aloo, he had to get to the square. Although it would be busy with hostiles—like the spaceport—it had to be better than asking every cargo bay guard on every ship where they were heading.

As he walked in the direction of the square, Seb looked over at the fighting pit. The first time he'd seen it since he'd escaped the Shadow Order's base, he felt nothing. No giddiness, no pull towards it. Not only because Moses would find him in seconds if he entered there, but also because fighting for a pittance seemed like a lifetime ago. Maybe because he had enough violence in his life now—too much, in fact. Every few hours seemed to feature a fight with something. A snort of a laugh, he shook his head to himself. How had he ended up here?

A narrow alleyway led into the square. To look through it at the jostling space beyond sent Seb's heart racing. If they uncovered him in a place where he was so heavily outnumbered, it could be curtains. But he had to try. He had to do something other than run around the sewers being chased by Moses' bounty hunters.

As much as he could hide his face, Seb couldn't hide his form. At best, he could walk with a slight hunch to show a shape other than a typical human physique. Leaning into the pain he felt in his hip from falling over in the sewers, he moved with a tilt to the side.

At certain times of day, the square was the busiest place on Aloo. Seb had timed it so he walked into chaos. The middle of the day, the ships had their business to do before they took off again.

The tight press of creatures meant Seb always touched another being, no matter where he moved to. Every few seconds, a large brute would shove through the crowd, cutting a path and knocking beings over in its wake. The impact of the next one to pass through burned Seb's shoulder when it smashed into him, but it didn't knock him down.

A deep breath helped Seb keep his head. As much as he wanted to swing for it, even he knew he had to keep a lid on his rage at that point.

Besides, Seb had gone to the square for the whispers, not for the oafs looking to assert their authority. Each being in the place had their destination. Some were looking to catch a ride while the others were taking cargo there. The ones who were offering lifts advertised where they were heading as a repeated low murmur, over and over. The cumulative effect of the sounds buzzed like a swarm of bees. It would take a great effort to find the place he needed in amongst the chaos.

The reason for the square's existence was because most ships passed through Aloo with a cargo of one sort or another. If they could pick up a being and earn an extra few credits to take them where they were already heading, then it made sense to get the extra pay for the journey. The crew saw it as their tip. If the being looking for a ride out of there also had a cargo of their own, it was even better. A chance to earn on a load that didn't have to be registered to whoever owned the ship. Most ship owners didn't ride in their vessels. They simply bought them and used them to earn credits. If the captains and their crew could earn a bit on the side, very few beings begrudged them that.

It took a minute or two of milling through the crowd before Seb picked out the place names.

"Solsans."

"Grinth."

"Orch."

And on.

None of them were places Seb wanted to visit. But then he heard it. The name he'd been waiting for. He pulled the front of his hood aside to see the creature better. Another creature stepped forwards before Seb could. It took it up on the offer.

Just as Seb readied himself to follow the pair—a safe distance back so as not to reveal himself—he heard something say Carstic. A flashback to the mines caught him off guard and he looked at the creature who'd spoken.

A large insect, it had wide bulbous eyes on each side of its long, brilliant blue head. When it saw Seb, those eyes widened to the point where they looked like they could fall out. Still with his face on show, Seb had clearly helped the thing recognise the bounty in front of it.

As he stared at the greed now looking back at him, the walls of Seb's world seemed to close in around him.

CHAPTER 23

The insect pointed a shaking finger at Seb and opened its long mouth as it drew a breath. Before it could call out, Seb pulled back the left breast of his cloak to reveal the blaster in his top pocket. Where he'd once enjoyed fighting, he'd do whatever he could to avoid it now. Especially in the busy square.

Eyes still spread wide, the ugly being looked from Seb, down to his blaster, and back at Seb again. The creature's deliberation gave Seb the time he needed to close the distance between them.

The flaps of his hood covering his face again, his attention on the ground to be sure he remained hidden from every other being around him, Seb spoke in a low murmur so only the blue bug heard him. "You even think about giving me away and I'll kill you. Even if I don't get out of here, know that you won't either."

Silence.

"You got that?"

"Yep."

Seb lifted his head enough to look at the being again.

Where it had been a vibrant blue only a few seconds ago, the colour had left its skin, turning it pale.

Some creatures had their ship name on their clothes. As Seb stared down at the embroidered badge, he said, "Now I know you're on the *Conquest*. I promise you, I *will* find you if this comes back to me."

The insect continued to remain silent.

The more Seb spoke, the greater the chance of him giving himself away. So rather than level more threats on the ugly thing, he spun on his heel and headed out of the square. He knew where he needed to go, and thankfully the creatures he needed to follow were still in his line of sight.

The press of bodies made it hard to catch up with them, but Seb dropped his head and barged his way through. Now he knew he had a ride out of there, he couldn't let it get away.

CHAPTER 24

A small and unremarkable ship, Seb read the name painted on its body. *The Slip*. He watched the interaction between the passenger in the square and *The Slip*'s crew member who'd brought him back with him. The crew member struck an imposing sight. At least seven feet tall, it had broad shoulders, a thick rhino's horn in the centre of its face, grey skin, and blood-red eyes. A safe distance away, Seb made sure he blended into the crowd, and he made sure he kept his face hidden.

After a discussion that lasted no more than a few seconds, the being from the square looked *The Slip* up and down, shook its head, and walked away. Obviously not enough space to carry its cargo. Sometimes having a passenger with baggage didn't work out.

Seb watched the creature from the square disappear into the hustle and bustle of the spaceport before he stepped forward.

Keep your head, the female voice said to him just before he revealed himself.

It caught Seb off guard and he froze.

You can do this, but just keep a lid on it, okay? They may provoke you, especially when they see you're human.

Of course she was right. A nod to himself, Seb stepped from the crowd into the shadow cast by *The Slip*'s small body.

Two other beings were with the one who'd just returned from the square. They stood by the cargo bay's doors. Each a different species, but each of them larger and wider than Seb. They all looked his way, tense at his approach.

The one who'd returned from the square had black scars streaking its grey skin. "Who are you?"

But Seb didn't speak. Instead, he stared at them and kept his face hidden from their view.

A snort of frustration, the creature who spoke snapped its head up in a butting motion, showing the damage its horn could do. "I *said* who are you?"

A look from the rhino to its two henchmen on either side of it, Seb pulled his hood back.

All three creatures held semi-automatic blasters. All three of them snapped them up into their shoulders and pointed them Seb's way. They each closed one eye and watched him down the barrels of their weapons.

"What are you doing here, *human*?"

Again, Seb said nothing, his mum's words calming him down. The best way to keep his head had to be keeping his mouth shut.

The leader with the rhino horn stepped forward. It kept its gun raised, the stock of it pressed into its shoulder and cheek. It continued to aim it at him. It didn't speak, grinding its thick jaw and scowling. Although the edges of Seb's world blurred, he didn't let his gift take him over. The situation might have been tense, but he somehow knew it wouldn't kick off. As long as he kept his head.

"It's *him*," the guard on the leader's left said. It too had horns, but they were on the sides of its head and curled like those of a ram. "It's the *human* Moses has put a bounty on."

In the silence that followed the ram-creature's statement, Seb remained perfectly still. Sharp movements would no doubt see him killed. His heart pounded as if it wanted out of his chest. Maybe he should back away slowly and find another way. Although, what other way would there be out of there?

After what seemed to be an anxious look at its two colleagues, the rhino moved closer to Seb. It kept its blaster aimed at him as it reached out in his direction. It then slipped its large hand inside Seb's robe and removed his gun and sword. It put them in its own pockets. A second later, it found the mobile phone Buster had given him and took that too.

"I'll let you borrow those," Seb said, and the creature jumped backwards at his words. It kept its blaster raised and pointed at him. What had Moses said about him? Armed and dangerous? Fighting skills to be an arena champion?

"Where did you get this sword from?"

"You recognise it?"

"Just answer the question." As assertive as it tried to be, the beast failed to hide its nerves, its voice shaking. Moses must have really laid it on thick about Seb.

"I found it on an unconscious cargo bay guard." Seb made a point of looking at the other two before returning his attention to their leader. "It could have remained conscious had it not provoked me."

Seb couldn't help but smile to watch the rhino creature's throat bob when it swallowed.

The other of the three guards—the hornless one—said, "We should take him to the captain."

Thankfully they'd said that rather than taking him to Moses. He'd be able to help the captain see reason.

CHAPTER 25

The same reaction he got wherever he went in Aloo, Seb watched the captain of *The Slip* twist in his presence as if his simply being there turned the air rancid. Then he scowled pure contempt at him. A mandulu! They were every-where. It would be hard to keep his mouth shut with this one. *You can do it,* the voice said.

So close Seb could feel his body heat, the mandulu looked him up and down. "You're the one Moses is looking for, aren't you?"

"Before you hand me in and claim your reward," Seb said, staring at the beast's fat and weak chin, "can you check my back pocket? I don't want to reach for it in case you think I'm trying to grab a weapon."

The captain looked at the rhino guard and nodded in Seb's direction. "Go on, then."

The rhino paused, clearly not on board with the idea of getting close to Seb again. But when the mandulu glared at it, it clearly realised it had no other option.

Seb lifted his robe to make it easier for the brute and winked at it. "Now don't get frisky, okay?"

The creature snorted at him and rammed its hand into his back pocket so hard it nearly dragged his trousers down with the force.

It retrieved the card and handed it to the mandulu. The captain of the ship stared at it for a few seconds. The silence held as it pulled a small light from its pocket and ran it over the plastic rectangle. The circular emblem with the submarine in the middle of it lit up. After a heavy sigh, the mandulu said, "Why didn't you tell them you had this?"

A look at the rhino, Seb shrugged. "Didn't trust them enough to reveal it. I wanted to get to you first."

The rhino scowled but didn't reply.

"Besides, it wouldn't have been anywhere near as fun. Might as well wind the monkeys up before I get to see the organ grinder, eh?"

The captain stared at Seb.

"So this card trumps the reward Moses will pay for me?"

"*It* doesn't trump it," the captain said, "it's just a piece of plastic."

Had Owsk sold him out? A slight quickening of his pulse, Seb looked at the captain, the rhino, and back to the captain. Despite his urge to ball his metal fists in defence, he resisted, opting for "*Huh*?" instead.

Silence. The rhino stepped closer to Seb, clearly desperate for a chance to attack him.

Another weary sigh, the captain said, "However, my obligation to the card and, by extension of this card, to *you*, trumps it."

"That'll do." Seb relaxed, smiled, and held an open palm in the direction of the rhino creature. "I've let you hold my weapons and phone for long enough now. Give them back before you get any ideas of keeping them."

After watching his head guard hand Seb his weapons back, the captain said, "Where do you want to go?"

"The same place you're going to."

"You know where we're going?"

"Yep. I heard that simpleton advertise it in the square."

The rhino bristled, but Seb only had a peripheral awareness of it because he remained fixed on the captain.

Another pause, the captain appeared to be searching for some reason within himself to say no. But he also looked like he knew he couldn't, regardless of how rich Moses' credits would make him. "*Fine*," he finally said before calling out through the ship at unseen crew members, "Let's get ready to depart for Danu."

CHAPTER 26

Maybe Seb's memory of the house came from when he used to be happy. A time when nothing mattered but water fights with Davey and making sure they were home for dinner. Maybe it looked this bad when he'd seen it last and he'd been too close to it to notice. Maybe the time he'd been away had been enough to take its bite from the rickety structure. Completely empty since his dad had died, even basic maintenance would have stood it in better stead. Whatever the reason, now that he stood in front of his dad's old wooden house, it looked ready to collapse with exhaustion.

The winds on Aloo—especially on the docks—had been hard to cope with. The strength of the breeze on Danu went to a whole other level. The elements crashed so hard into Seb, he struggled to remain in the same spot. Despite the bright, early morning sunshine, the gales brought a bitter chill with them. As much as he hugged himself against the onslaught, the cold ran straight to his bones.

When he got to the doorstep of his dad's old house, Seb reached up and knocked. The rickety old door shook with the impact and the sound ran into what would undoubtedly be an empty house beyond. Why wouldn't it be? His dad had died years ago. But it didn't matter that Seb now had his name on the deeds. The house would always belong to his father.

No response, of course, yet Seb still remained there, waiting. The time when Officer Logan brought him back for fighting ran through his mind. He'd stood in exactly the same spot while his dad's old work colleague gave his dad what turned out to be the last true disappointment in a long line of disappointments. It had been the day his dad had revealed his prognosis.

The tall Officer Logan, although kind, remained loyal to Seb's dad from the days when they were on the force together. Because Seb got into so much trouble from fighting, that relationship often worked in his favour. Sure, he sugar-coated nothing when speaking to his dad, but Officer Logan had moved mountains to keep Seb from spending any time in jail. Bad enough they had Davey locked up.

At least fifteen minutes had passed since the taxi had dropped Seb off. He'd been outside for so long, staring at the house, that the sand in the wind burned the right side of his face. He either needed to turn around while he waited for someone to answer the door, or accept his reluctance as procrastination to help him avoid the pain buried deep inside him. At some point he'd have to cross the threshold.

Orphaned over two years ago at the age of twenty-four, no matter how long Seb waited outside, that wouldn't change. Yet he still didn't enter the place. The storm shutters on the outside of the house were closed. The generator was off. The only things living inside the house would be snakes, lizards, and spiders. The spiders and lizards he could cope with. A shudder snapped through him to think of some of the snakes they encountered this far out of town.

Seb finally leaned down and lifted the rock by the front

door. Heavier than he remembered it, the rough surface scratched his fingertips and he almost dropped it.

Several hard-shelled insects scattered as Seb tossed the rock to one side, leaving the copper key bug-free for him to retrieve. Not even the insects would give him an excuse to avoid going in.

A shake ran through Seb as he stabbed the key at the lock, missing the hole several times like a drunkard returning from a night out. When he finally got it in, he twisted it, the mechanism gritty like most things on Danu. The door fell open, the old hinges groaning with its movement. The sound called along the dusty and deserted hallway. "Hopefully it'll scare the snakes off," he said, loud enough so he did the job if the hinges hadn't. Another cringe twisted through him.

Once inside, Seb closed the door, cutting off the howling wind and blocking out most of the light. The wind shutters had been fastened tight, so the only illumination came through the many cracks in the building's shell. The place smelled of dust and sand. Maybe he'd stay long enough to do something about it. Maybe he could tidy up a little. Not likely though.

Because he still wore his cloak, albeit with the hood down, Seb reached into its pocket and felt for the phone Buster had given him. By Buster's reckoning, he still had a few days before it rang.

A deep breath as if he were about to jump into an ice bath, Seb's heart sped away from him as he delved deeper into his dad's old house. The sand on the wooden floorboards crunched beneath his every step, letting the ghosts know he'd returned. As much as his memories of his dad made him feel like crap, he had to remember he was a good man. They rarely saw eye to eye, but he wanted what he believed to be the best for his boys. He ended up with what he believed to be the absolute worst. Seb sighed. Who could blame him for being disappointed?

Seb walked around the house, opening the windows and then shutters in turn. Each time he got a sandblasting as he threw the shutters wide, the bright glare from outside momentarily dazzling him. Only a few seconds before he closed the windows, but enough to fill the house with a rush of sandy air. At least it helped clear out what smelled like years' worth of stagnation.

When he opened each window, Seb also scanned the horizon for the creature who'd tailed him on Aloo. If Moses had hired a bounty hunter, they would be among the best at what they did. Even if they hadn't ridden on *The Slip* with him, it wouldn't take them long to track him down. The second he lowered his guard would be the second he regretted it.

A chill deep in his bones from spending too much time outside, Seb went to the front room next. The basket next to the fireplace overflowed with wood. His dad never liked to run out of anything. The cupboards always had two of each item because he liked to have a spare. The number of times he'd shouted at Seb for not telling him when he'd used up the last jar or can of whatever product they'd run out of. The slightest hint of a smile lifted the sides of Seb's mouth to think about it now.

Even if some of the other supplies in the house ran out, firewood had always been a constant. In fact, Seb had never seen the bucket go any lower than three-quarters full. If any of the family passed comment, they'd be reminded of the great sandstorm years previously that meant no one could get out of their houses for days. Several old people had died because of the cold.

"Yeah, Dad," Seb said, continuing the argument in the

empty house, "but they were old, and it was twenty-five years ago. So, no, I don't remember it." The sound of his own voice echoed through the place. It highlighted his forced tone of trying to find humour where he had none. He swallowed a gritty gulp, grief adding to the burn in his throat.

It took about fifteen minutes before the fire kicked out enough heat for Seb to remove his cloak. For a moment, he considered burning it. Horrible thing, and he'd paid through the nose for it. Instead, he threw it on the sofa and fell backwards into his dad's chair. Dust kicked up from not being used for years, but after a minute it settled and Seb revelled in the warmth of the open fire and his position directly in front of it.

Exhaustion ran through Seb's veins, his muscles turning to lead as he listened to the hiss, pop, and crackle of the fire. The flames danced for him, hypnotising him and taking some of his many worries away. Buster would call at some point. Until then, he just had to wait.

Seb looked around the room at the photographs on display. Always fair, there were two pictures of him and two pictures of his brother, Davey, the only remaining family member not dead. Every other photo of the twenty-three was of his mum. As he looked at them, the details of each image faded away, blurring behind his spread of tears. He'd barely had a chance to get to know her. He barely knew himself at nine years old.

Time passed, Seb's cheeks turning sodden with his tears. He had to remember why he'd come back to the house. Owsk had told Seb about the prophecy. One of the many beings to tell him what they saw. He had something in his blood. Something that meant he was destined for great things. The gift had been passed down from his mother. That was why he'd come back to his dad's home. Surely he'd find something there.

Seb's gaze returned to the only family photo in the room. Above the fireplace, it had his mum and dad in the middle. Davey sat on one side, him on the other. It showed a time when they were happy. A time he didn't remember.

Maybe Seb should visit Davey. His only remaining relative, and someone who shared his blood. Maybe Seb's only part in the prophecy would be to help his brother realise his full potential. Maybe Davey carried the special talents buried deep within their mother's genes.

Whenever Seb had wanted to visit Davey in the past, he'd always been told no. But he hadn't tried for years. Now he'd returned to Danu, he had to give it another go.

Yes, you should.

The voice caught Seb off guard and he looked around the room. "Mum?"

Nothing.

"Should I go and see Davey?"

Yes.

As much as he tried to hold them back, Seb's tears returned in a heavy wave.

CHAPTER 27

I t took several hours and a river of tears before Seb felt like he could move again. Once he'd started crying, it took a huge effort to stop. The fire now glowed, the roaring flames of a few hours ago just a distant memory buried in the embers. Although his body still ached, it had done him good to rest up.

For the entire time Seb had sat in his dad's seat by the fire, he'd waited. He'd waited for the energy and resolve to get up, but more importantly, he'd waited for the voice to return to him. He'd even muttered, "Mum?" once or twice in the hope she'd say something. She didn't.

Seb put his hand on his stomach when it rumbled. He couldn't remember the last time he ate. Would there still be food in the kitchen? Probably. Two of everything. But would it still be edible?

At only twenty-seven, Seb shocked himself when he groaned as he stood up out of his seat. His dad had always said one of the first signs he was getting old came when he started making noises to help him stand up. The thought of it made him smile, but a maudlin pang rode on the back of it.

Like the rest of the house, the kitchen hadn't been touched since Seb had been there last. Now he had daylight streaming through the un-shuttered windows, he saw the dust motes dancing in the air. They ran up his nose, his eyes watering again before he sneezed several times in quick succession. The sound of it went off in the quiet house like a bomb.

Dried-up mowgrove fruit sat in the fruit bowl. Utterly inedible by now. When his dad had told him his prognosis, he'd been eating one. The nauseous lump returned to his stomach and threatened to drag him under again. But he drew a deep breath, straightened his posture, and pulled his shoulders back. He needed to keep going. Eat, go and see Davey, and then make a choice from there. Maybe Davey had an idea on how he could find out who their mum had been. What they'd inherited from her genetics.

True to form, the cupboards had two of everything in them. Two tins of beans. Two tins of peaches. Two packets of dried noodles with squoch. Seb reached up and pulled both tins of peaches down, looking over his shoulders from where he could feel his dad's eyes on him. "We've got no peaches left, Dad, you'll need to order some more," he said, his voice dying in the house's stillness.

The use by date on the side of the tin showed they had a few years before they went bad, so Seb removed the lid, bent it so he could use it as a spoon, and scooped the fruit from the can.

The peaches were in syrup. The thick sugary hit lit up Seb's taste buds and made his mouth water.

Each bite of the plump slices exploded in Seb's mouth. Then he looked at his dad's safe and the enjoyment of his experience dulled. It had always been there, in plain sight. It had been embedded in the wall for as long as they'd lived in the house. But his dad had never revealed its contents, and Seb had never dared ask. Not the most communicative of relationships.

And now, even if Seb had wanted to get inside the safe, he wouldn't know where to start looking for the key.

Two tins of peaches down, and although Seb enjoyed the sweet aftertaste, his stomach hadn't got the message that he'd eaten anything yet. A look back in the cupboard. The noodles would be edible, but no more tasty than they'd always been. Whenever he'd eaten them in the past, they left him with a foul aftertaste and the need to drink about seven gallons of water to combat the salty hit. They were a last resort kind of food. The sort of food that tasted great when he was a teenager.

Before Seb could take the beans from the cupboard, the groan of the front door's hinges enquired through the house. Is anybody home?

The sound spiked Seb's pulse and he froze for a moment, looking in the direction of the front door, but unable to see it from where he stood.

Because Seb had left his cloak and weapons in the front room, he balled his metal fists instead and shook his head to himself. Not another damn fight. A deep breath to slow his world down, he then ran across the wooden floor on tiptoes. He pressed his back against the wall next to the kitchen door and held his breath to listen.

Footsteps walked up the hallway towards him, the crunch of sand beneath them. The floorboards creaked, almost as if the old house let out a weary sigh at being trodden on.

The steps of the intruder were heavy against the floor. Whoever came at him at that moment sounded like they were large enough to cause him trouble. They also sounded like they didn't expect anyone else to be there.

As the intruder drew closer, Seb's pulse kicked through him, adrenaline building up, ready to be spent. Fight or flight. He rarely ran.

One last deep breath to slip into slow motion, Seb then jumped from his hiding place, screamed as he kicked the kitchen door wide open, and rushed forward with his fists raised.

CHAPTER 28

"Logan?" Seb said as he came face to face with his dad's old best friend. Good job he had the ability to slow down time. Had he not been viewing events through his slow motion lens, he would have swung first and asked questions later. Even with his abilities, he only just managed to hold back.

In the face of his dad's friend's kind and calm assessment, Seb said, "What are you doing here?"

At first, Logan shrugged. He opened his mouth several times as if to speak and then must have thought better of it. A few more seconds passed before he finally said, "I was just checking the place out."

A snort of a laugh—a loud burst of noise in the quiet house—Seb then said, "What, you were just passing? Come on, I find that a little hard to believe. The desert is the kind of place you come to kill yourself, not somewhere you go for a scenic drive."

"I've been checking on the place when I can. I think your dad would have wanted me to. I want to make sure it hasn't been robbed or taken over by squatters. When I saw smoke …"

Seb looked through the living room's door at the glowing fire. He shrugged. "That makes sense."

As he looked Seb up and down, Logan said, "So what have you been up to, boy?"

Older and wiser than he'd been when he'd last seen Logan, Seb tensed at being called *boy,* but he let it slide. Very few people could call him that. In fact, with his dad gone, probably just one person could call him that and get away with it.

CHAPTER 29

The fire popped and crackled. Seb had put more logs on a few hours previously. The flames had now sunk into the glowing embers that had been there when Logan arrived. It served as the only measure of how long they'd talked for because there were no clocks in the room.

It made sense to tell Logan everything. Well, nearly everything. Seb had told him about the Shadow Order, about SA—he'd told him a lot about SA, his infatuation with her not missed by Logan. He'd spoken about the war with the Crimson Countess and how they'd lost Gurt. He'd also told him about Moses and what he'd probably face if he ever returned to the Shadow Order's base. However, he hadn't told Logan about the voice of his mother in his head, and he hadn't told him about the prophecy. As kind as Logan was, believing such crazy nonsense would be a stretch too far even for his generous heart.

For the entire time Seb had spoken to him for, Logan sat back on the sofa next to Seb's ratty, old cape and listened. He laughed when Seb told him what he'd paid for the garment.

"You're doing the right thing, boy," Logan said. "You've grown up so much since you left. Your dad would be proud."

The statement sideswiped Seb, his grief springing on him without warning. It took a few seconds for him to gulp it back down and say, "But I fight a lot more."

"You're fighting for the *right* reasons. He'd see that."

Seb stood up and walked over to the nearest window. While peering out into the dusty Danu desert, searching for signs of Moses' bounty hunter, he said, "I need to go and see Davey."

The slight smile both on Logan's lips and in his eyes vanished. His tone turned sombre. "Are you sure?"

A deep inhale of the smokey air, the charred taste of it catching in his throat, Seb nodded. "I haven't seen him for years. Can you get me visitation rights on the quiet? I'm sure I could do it officially, but that'll leave a trail for Moses to find."

For the next few seconds, the only sound came from the wind outside and the fire as it popped and fizzed.

Logan finally nodded. "Yep, I can do it. I *shouldn't,* but I will. I don't see much harm in it. You're only visiting your brother, right?"

"Right." Seb then said, "Oh, and Davey's always said he doesn't want visitors."

The smile returned to Logan's kind face. "Don't worry about that. I'll sort it out."

CHAPTER 30

I t only took a few hours for Logan to arrange Seb's prison visit, and another hour for them to get there. The amount of service he'd given Danu's police force had to have some advantages. The old frant had certainly been chewed up and spat back out again by the job. They owed him a favour or two.

The plastic chair had no padding and Seb wriggled as he sat on it, trying to find comfort where he wouldn't be able to. The awkward twist emanated from his core, and no amount of shuffling would relieve it. He sat at a booth, wooden panels on either side of him and reinforced glass in front. A phone hung in a receiver, and a chair like the one he perched on sat empty on the other side of the glass. No doubt the ones on that side had been bolted to the floor. Who knew what the prisoners would do with a weapon like that?

Booths similar to the one Seb sat in ran away from him in both directions. Many of the beings on Seb's side had phones to their ears and were talking to their loved ones opposite them. How many years had their relationship had a glass barrier between it? How many more did they have left?

A strong smell of bleach hung in the air. Typical government facility, they'd sterilised the personality out of the place. Unfortunately for Seb, the bleach hadn't been applied thickly enough to mask the smell of what must have been a child's full nappy. No children in there at that moment, the small beast must have left the stench as a parting gift to whoever came in after them. Or maybe an infantile *screw you* to the jailers.

Every time the door on the other side of the glass opened, Seb looked up. Six guards by it, two mandulus, two frants, and he didn't know what the other two were. They all held semi-automatic blasters, wore deep frowns, and barely blinked as they watched the prisoners for signs of trouble. They looked like they'd be glad of an excuse to exert their will.

So far, the door had let through seven or eight prisoners. Each time Seb's stomach had turned a backflip in anticipation. But none of them were Davey. It had been years since he'd seen him. Would he even recognise him now?

An occasional look over his shoulder at the door he'd entered through, Seb could still feel the attention of something. Maybe Moses' bounty hunter had caught up with him. Hopefully they'd left Logan alone if they had. Not that he needed to worry about him. The old cop could look after himself. He'd opted to wait in the car outside. He had Buster's satellite phone with him. There would have been no way the prison would have let the device in. Although harmless, the large case could have contained anything. Seb couldn't afford to leave it unattended.

When the door leading to the prison clicked again, Seb saw the next person enter and the air left his lungs. He whispered, "Davey?"

Heavy bags beneath his sunken eyes, Davey fixed his dark stare on Seb and strode over to the booth.

Seb physically recoiled from his big brother's approach.

The years in prison looked to have put decades on him. It had turned him into a jaded version of their father.

When Davey sat down, he stared at Seb with no change of expression and picked up the phone on his side.

Seb did the same and then pressed his palm against the cold glass separating them. He listened to his brother's heavy breaths. A cheap phone, the quality left a lot to be desired. For a few seconds he could do no more than stare back at his brother. How had he turned into their father so quickly?

Finally, Seb said, "You look like shit, Davey."

The stern expression broke and Davey smiled, his once boyish face now a mess of wrinkles. His teeth had turned brown and he wore a thick stubble. He looked like he'd been sleeping rough for all the time he'd been locked up. His voice rumbled through the receiver's speaker. "Thanks, little bro. I love you too."

The flash of humanity that ran through his brother's withered face helped Seb relax a little and he shrugged. "You know me."

"I used to."

The words cut to Seb's heart, his resentment spilling out. "*You* were the one who kept rejecting my requests to visit."

A lazy roll of his eyes, Davey said, "I didn't even get a request this time. More a summons."

Seb didn't reply to that. Logan probably wouldn't get in trouble for arranging a visit, but best to keep it close to his chest anyway.

After a weary sigh, Davey said, "So Dad's gone."

It disarmed Seb. The prison, Davey's resemblance to their

father, the prophecy, his mother's voice. Tears itched his eyes and the haggard version of a brother he once knew blurred.

"Come on, bro," Davey said. "It's okay. He had enough time to tell us how much of a disappointment we were. He'll be happy in heaven, or hell, or wherever he's ended up."

"Probably being a pain in someone's arse somewhere," Seb said with a smile.

Davey smiled back. "Wherever he is, I bet he's making sure they have two of everything in the cupboards!"

Seb and Davey laughed before the mood fell again. Davey looked straight into Seb's eyes. "He used to visit, you know?"

"He *did*?"

"Yeah. Every week without fail."

While shaking his head, Seb frowned at his brother. "Why didn't he tell me?"

"I asked him not to. I didn't want you coming here. If you knew he visited, you'd insist on doing the same. If you found out, I would have cut off his visits too, and I didn't want to do that. He didn't want me to do that."

"So he kept your secret."

"Yeah."

"Dad wouldn't *ever* speak about you. And when he did, it was like you were dead to him."

"He had to do that to cover the lie. He asked me every week if he could tell you he came, but I didn't want you seeing me like this. I asked a lot of him, and he bore the burden of your resentment. It's me you should be angry with, not him."

The stinging sensation returned to Seb's eyeballs and his bottom lip buckled. Although he drew a deep breath, it did little to subdue his grief. "I felt like I hated him a lot of the time."

"And that killed him. I didn't want to see you, not even when summoned today, but I thought it was important you knew it wasn't his call."

So much to catch up on, but in the next few days Buster's phone would ring and Seb would be gone again. "I don't know how long I'm going to be here," Seb said. "I want to come and see you regularly like Dad did. We have a lot to talk about."

But Davey shook his head. "Prison's not fun. Especially for a cop killer. They hardly roll out the red carpet for you. If I ever do get out of here, it'll be when I'm old and frail. It'll probably be when I've lost my marbles and control of my bowels. They'll free me because they won't want to wipe my arse for me anymore. I'll die in a gutter somewhere because I probably won't even know my own name. They would have taken their pound of flesh and then some by that time, so why waste the resources on me?"

At that moment, the voice of his mother came to Seb. *Be strong.* He drew a breath to tell Davey what he'd learned about the prophecy, but Davey cut him off.

"I am glad you came."

"You are?"

"Yeah, I know I just made a fuss about it, but I wanted to see my last remaining relative one final time. That's what I've been waiting for. I didn't know if you'd ever try to come here again, but I felt like I owed it to you to be here if you did. I owed it to Dad and your memory of him. I would have waited for however long it took to make sure you knew the truth."

The lump in Seb's throat burned and he laughed through it. "Even if that meant shitting yourself in a gutter as an OAP?"

Davey smiled.

"You're my brother," Seb then said, "of course I would

try again." Then the words caught up with him. "What do you mean, *one last time?*"

Instead of answering him, Davey replaced the phone on his side of the glass. A heavy *click* popped in Seb's ear from where the line got cut off.

Seb kept his hand pressed against the cold and clear barrier between them, a gesture his brother hadn't returned. He pressed the glass as if he could push through it.

"I love you, little brother," Davey called back over his shoulder as he stood up and walked away. "Get the hell away from this place and find a better life. Danu's the armpit of the galaxy. It has nothing to offer."

"Davey ..." Seb's words died as he watched Davey run full tilt at the group of guards on his side of the glass. He pulled a shiv from out of the back of his trousers and he looked ready to use it. Before he'd made it to the first guard, three of them raised their blasters and let rip. The red laser fire hit Davey in several places, sending his arms kicking away from him. One shot ran through his face and dragged a spray of blood out the back of his head. Some of the spray hit the glass in front of Seb and he flinched away from it as if it might cover him.

Seb would have shouted if he'd had it in him. Instead, he remained frozen to the spot while the guards on the other side of the glass crowded around Davey's dead body, their weapons pointing down at him just in case they'd misjudged his current state.

You need to get out of there, Seb. If you stay, they'll ques-tion you, and Moses will see your name pop up on a system somewhere. Get out now.

Were he not in a room full of people, Seb might have replied to his mum's voice. Instead, he pushed off the desk to help him stand up. He felt drunk as he walked out of the room, his legs weak, his vision blurred.

The only thing keeping Seb going as he stumbled out of there was the voice of his mother. *I love you, Seb. You have a new family around you now. Be with them and fulfil your potential.*

CHAPTER 31

"He said he let Dad visit, but he wouldn't ever let me," Seb said as Logan drove them back to his dad's house. The car bounced with the undulations in Danu's barren wasteland. The small cushion of air it rode on did little to make the ride any smoother than if they'd had wheels. In fact, it would have coped better with wheels. It seemed that whenever Logan's old police car passed over a particularly nasty bump, it would bob for the next quarter of a mile.

Logan kept his attention through the front windscreen. The sun had started to set on the horizon, a red glow slowly taking over the sky. "What would you have had him do?"

"I think he should have told me. It's the right thing to do. He should have let *me* make the choice about what was good for me."

"Like you've done with your Shadow Order friends?"

Seb looked at the older man and ground his jaw. Rage and despair ran through him in equal measure after what he'd just witnessed. His voice cracked when he said, "That's different."

"How? You think you know better than them? That you

know what's good for them, but others don't know what's good for you?"

Another look at his dad's oldest friend, the tall frant still frowned as he stared ahead. He sat hunched over the steering wheel. Something about his demeanour didn't ring true. "You *knew*," Seb said. He pointed at the older being. "You knew about Dad's visits."

"Of course I did."

"Then why didn't you tell me?"

"Because he didn't want me to."

To stop the vicious torrent rushing from his mouth, Seb paused and looked out of the window next to him at the sandy landscape. His pulse raced while he watched the barren wasteland fly past. The sun might have hung much lower in the sky, but it still shone bright and he had to squint against its glare. But he couldn't be angry with Logan. The old creature hadn't done anything wrong. In a much quieter voice than before, he said, "I've not got anyone left, Logan."

The old man reached across with his large left hand and squeezed Seb's shoulder. He looked at him for the first time since they'd been in the car. "You've got your friends still. They sound like they love you." A snort of a laugh, he added, "Although I don't know why."

Despite the gravity of what had happened, Seb smiled.

"Sometimes we make what we think are the best decisions," Logan said. "From what I've seen, they rarely are. Maybe we're trying to protect those we love, but maybe we're trying to protect ourselves. Maybe Davey hurt too much to then see his sadness staring back at him through his brother's eyes. Maybe you need to put yourself in his shoes and allow him that one freedom he had left, the freedom of making a choice about who came to visit him."

Seb's bottom lip buckled. "The first thing I said to him

was that he looked old. Of all the things, I told him he looked like shit."

Logan didn't reply.

Before he could think twice about it, Seb said, "I think I hear Mum's voice."

The hum of the car filled the silence between them as Logan turned to look at Seb again.

"Since I've broken out of the Shadow Order's base, I've started hearing the voice of a woman in my head. I think it's Mum."

Logan said nothing.

"You think I'm crazy?"

"No."

"You don't believe me?"

"I believe you hear a voice in your head."

Another deep inhale, Seb then forced the words out. "I've been told I'm the chosen one, Logan. *Many* times. That I have the blood of someone great in me. I think it's Mum's blood. I think that's why she's talking to me now. I think she's guiding me to wherever it is I need to go."

The sound of air rushed over the hover car. When Seb looked at Logan, he saw a frown on his long face and said, "You know something, don't you?"

Before Logan could reply, something came crashing from the sky on Seb's left. He looked through the window to watch a large blur slam down against the dusty plains beside them.

The car snaked from the shockwave and Logan fought to pull it under control.

The dust settled to reveal a mech. Easily ten metres tall, it stood in the low sun, the light bouncing off its chrome body. It had no markings to show where it had come from. It didn't need any. "Stop the car," Seb said.

Nothing.

"*Please,* Logan, stop the car now."

"It's from the Shadow Order?" the old man asked.

"Yep. I've felt something following me since I got away from the base. I can't keep running from it. Besides, if we're going to fight, it's best we do it here, away from civilisation."

Although he looked reluctant, Logan slowed the vehicle to a halt. They were in the shadow of the vast mech, which watched them the entire time.

Seb opened the door, the sandy Danu winds flying into the dusty car. One foot out, he turned to his dad's best friend. "Wait here. I can handle this."

CHAPTER 32

Twice the size of the mech he'd fought at the Shadow Order's base, Seb's heart raced to look up at the huge chrome beast. Two arms, two legs, a head with all the features of a human face crudely depicted on it, and not much else. Its shiny body didn't give anything away, the lowering evening sun glistening off the mech's chrome frame. It magnified the glare, dazzling Seb as he searched it for a weakness.

Then the robot charged forward, closing down the distance between them with its heavy steps.

Seb thrust his arms out to the sides just to keep his balance. The vibration of the mech's movement threatened to throw him to the ground.

The world now in slow motion, Seb watched the large machine rush at him, the strong winds buffeting his ears. The mech raised a huge right fist, ready to strike.

The beast might have been big, but what it had in power, it lost in speed. The punch came from a mile away, the expressionless brute driving it down into the ground.

With plenty of time to get out of the way, Seb avoided the

first blow. The impact sent a blast of rock shards towards him and he raised his arms in front of his face to protect against the stinging assault.

Several pieces of shrapnel cut into Seb's forearms. Thankfully he avoided the worst of it, and at least he kept his face covered. The beast might have been slow, but he couldn't fight it blind.

Seb tasted sand on the back of his dry throat. Despite the cold wind, sweat itched his armpits and around his collar.

The mech pulled its fist up again and spun on Seb, its upper body moving while its legs remained stationary. It then jumped to allow its bottom half to spin around to catch up with its top. It sent a series of jackhammer blows against the ground. It might not be able to hit Seb, but it could try to take away his ability to evade it.

Although Seb rode out the first few shocks, the third one robbed him of his footing. While he scrambled away from the follow-up impacts, he bounced around every time a metal fist connected. A pea on a drum, he just about managed to stay out of the gargantuan's reach, every punch slamming down closer to him than the one before it.

The mech paused and Seb took his opportunity. He charged over the uneven and dusty ground at it. A gap large enough to drive a car between its legs, he ran through it and punched its calf like he had with the last one he'd come up against. Although this time, the brute's chrome body threw his punch back at him as if he'd just whacked something made from rubber.

The mech jumped into the air, spun around, and landed with another earth-shaking *boom*. It charged at Seb again.

The vibrations of the mech's stampede ran through Seb and blurred his vision, but he managed to remain upright.

When the mech drew close, it wound its right boot back.

Seb dived out of the way, the boat of a foot sailing just over his head. It might have missed him, but the rush of air from the attack sent Seb rolling away from it.

Sweat ran into Seb's eyes, but he didn't stop to rub them as he got back to his feet. Instead, he jumped backwards, avoiding a heavy stamp from the mech just in front of him. It shook the planet as if it could crack it, and lifted him several feet in the air.

Despite having the wind driven from his body when he crashed down again, Seb jumped up and drove several punches against the top of the mech's foot. It had gone down so hard, it had sunk into Danu's dusty, rocky landscape. Again, the resilience of the mech's chrome shell rejected his attack.

Exhausted, hot, and with the taste of sand clogging his throat, Seb gulped and stared at the large robot. There had to be some way to beat it. Then he caught sight of something. Around the brute's wrists, he saw the slightest of lines. A shimmering line. A weak spot!

This time Seb waited nearby to encourage the beast's attack. He dodged the first punch, then the second. When the third landed, he jumped in time to stop the vibrations through the ground unsettling him, and he struck the mech's right wrist.

What had been a line of potential weakness now opened as a slight crack, revealing the wires within the behemoth.

The mech—its expression as cold as ever—peered down at Seb, clasped its two large hands together and raised them above its head. It then brought them crashing down at him.

Again, the beast moved too slowly to make contact, but the vibration through the ground knocked Seb over again. He swung at the brute's wrists as he fell, but came nowhere near hitting it.

Before Seb could recover, another punch crashed into the ground. It missed again.

Seb rolled away, the rocky plains digging into him all over his body. He ran around the right side of the brute, tempting it to swing for him.

As he'd hoped, the brute tried to hit him again. Maybe the pilot saw Seb's plan. It tried a different approach. Instead of punching down, it swung for him, its fist running about a metre above the ground.

As slow as every other attack it aimed at him, Seb jumped aside. The fist passed him and he swung for the wrist. His hard blow made contact, detaching the hand from the arm, flinging the fist away from the large beast.

Both Seb and the mech paused to watch the huge metal body part fly through the air.

The relief Seb felt at finding the mech's vulnerability lasted less than a second. His body sank as he followed the fist's trajectory, his stomach turning over against itself.

One of the times where he hated his slow motion, Seb had to live every painful second of the metal object's wide arc. It only had one destination.

Before Seb could shout "Logan", the fist had landed on his car, crushing it like a bug beneath a boot heel.

The shock forced an involuntary gasp from Seb, and before he could say anything else, the crushed vehicle exploded into a ball of flames, the air lighting up with a loud *whoosh!* The force of the blast knocked him over with a wall of fierce heat.

CHAPTER 33

For a few seconds, Seb remained sitting down, unable to move as he stared at the burning wreck of Logan's car. It felt like every muscle in his body had fallen limp. Logan wouldn't have gotten dragged into this if it wasn't for him.

The black mushroom cloud dissipated, driven skyward on the back of tall orange flames. Despite needing some form of hope, nothing could have survived the twisted wreck the car had become.

A *whoosh* of hydraulics caught Seb's attention and he spun in the direction of the large mech. It remained in the same spot, but a vertical slit had opened up down the centre of it, running in a line from the top of its head all the way to its crotch. The join that looked so obvious now hadn't been there just seconds ago. As the split spread wider, it reminded him of a huge metal sarcophagus.

Seb stared into the mech and noticed spinning cogs and firing pistons. But he didn't watch their synchronised dance as they pushed the robot's two halves wider. Instead, he stared at the helmeted pilot. When she removed her lid, he ground his jaw and clenched his steel fists. "Reyes."

Even with his world in slow motion, Seb didn't give himself a moment to think. Instead, he yelled so loudly it tore at his throat as he ran at the mech. "What have you done?"

Because Reyes' cockpit sat in the centre of the mech at an elevated position of about three to four metres from the ground, metal stairs folded out of the large thing to let her down. Seb didn't stop running when he got to them, his feet hammering a loud beat. So much chrome, the sun continued to dazzle him, but he squinted through it and focused all of his rage on Reyes at the top of them.

By the time Seb had climbed the staircase, Reyes had unstrapped from the cockpit. She pressed her hands together as if in prayer, her face wincing at his fury. "I'm so sorry, Seb, I didn't mean for that to happen. Moses sent me here to bring you back, not to kill anyone."

But Seb had no words for her. Instead, he grabbed the front of her shirt, pulled her the rest of the way from the cockpit, and threw her off the stairs to the sandy ground below.

Although Reyes screamed on the way down, something else took Seb's attention. It started as a small pip. His jaw fell loose and he stepped away, glancing back at his path down the stairs so he didn't fall. As the pulse grew louder, he looked into the cockpit at the glowing red light. It blinked in time with the noise and brightened with the increasing sound. Why hadn't he thought about it? The failsafe if the pilot got forcibly removed. He leapt in the direction he'd recently hurled Reyes.

The impact of landing on the hard and sandy ground ran up through Seb's body, balling as a stinging pain at the base of his back and throwing him forwards. He fell into a roll and turned over several times before he managed to get back to his feet, gritted his teeth through the pain, and sprinted away from the large chrome monster. The throbbing pulse chased him away. Reyes had already taken flight.

The explosion dwarfed the one that had just killed Logan. The blast hit Seb's back, throwing him face first onto the sandy ground.

A ball of fire swallowed the mech as Seb got to his feet and then dragged a gasping Reyes to hers. He held the front of her shirt in a clenched left fist and pulled back his right. "What the *hell* were you doing?"

Wide brown eyes stared at Seb. Reyes sweated and sand clung to her damp skin. "I didn't mean to hurt anybody."

"Why the hell were you trying to kill me, then?"

A shake of her head, she looked genuine when she said, "I *wasn't*. I knew I'd have to fight you just to get you to listen to me. You were hardly going to welcome me with open arms. I mean, look at it."

The flames had eased a little, revealing part of the large mech, which had already blackened from the explosion. Pain streaked through Seb's jaw as he stared at it and gritted his teeth. He then turned back on Reyes. "And what have you achieved? I'm still not going to come with you. Hell, I should cave your damn skull in and leave you for dead. I should send you back to Moses in a coffin."

"Please, Seb, trust me when I say I didn't mean to harm *anyone*. I couldn't think of any other way to get you to come back with me."

The more she spoke, the tighter it wound Seb. His fist ached from where he continued to clench it while holding it in front of her. "Mistake or not, I can't let it slide." But before he could swing for her, a voice stopped him.

"Now come on, Seb, is violence really necessary?"

Seb let go of the front of Reyes' shirt and turned to the

burning car. Or rather, the man in front of the burning car. "*Logan?*"

The old man—his long frame now carrying the slight stoop of his years—beamed a wizened grin. "Of course."

"But I thought you were in the car."

A look at the burning mech, Logan said, "When I saw the size of that *thing*, I knew I should wait elsewhere. Good job I didn't listen to you, eh?"

"Where did you wait?"

"I hid behind a large rock, far enough away from the car that I didn't get pulverised and then barbecued."

The sound of sirens ran across the Danu plains. Seb turned to look and saw a line of emergency vehicles heading their way. He looked back at Logan. "You think we should get out of here?"

A shake of his head, Logan said, "No, I'll get one of them to give us a lift back. We can say the mech was a test flight that went wrong, and that we've found the pilot. I'll back you up. It'll be a lot of paperwork, but seeing as no one's dead, we'll get away with it." The old man's brown eyes glowed when he looked at Reyes. "Hi, I'm Logan."

Reyes stared back at the old frant, her mouth wide with shock.

"She's called Reyes. You do realise she just tried to kill us, right?" Seb said.

A scowl at Seb, Reyes shook her head. "I *didn't*." She looked back to Logan, "I'm so sorry you nearly got hurt."

Logan shrugged. "Being in the police force, I've had a lot worse happen to me. At least it was an accident. I suppose you'd best come with us."

"Where?" Reyes said.

"Back to Seb's house."

"My dad's," Seb cut in. "And I didn't invite her."

"It's yours now, boy, and don't be a dick."

The sideways look from Reyes showed she hadn't missed Logan calling Seb *boy*. Dick he could cope with, but *boy?* ... and in front of her? Good job for her she decided to keep that observation to herself.

CHAPTER 34

As he stood in the front room of his dad's house—the smell of smoke still in the air from the fire he'd left burning when they went to visit Davey—Seb stared out of the window and watched the final police vehicle pull away. Logan stood on the porch and waved his colleague off as he disappeared into the swirling dust.

Silence hung between Seb and Reyes, the tension so thick it damn near choked him. The only sounds were the fierce winds outside and the stomp of Logan's heavy gait up the corridor towards them.

The second Logan entered the room, Seb said, "You should take Dad's old car."

A deep frown pressed down on Logan's soft brown eyes. He stared at Seb but didn't respond.

"You've lost your car because of me." A sharp glare at Reyes, Seb said, "Because of *her*."

Reyes looked like she wanted to speak. At least she had the good sense to keep her mouth shut. Seb continued. "Dad's has been outside doing nothing, and I have no intention of staying here. Especially now Davey's gone." Before Logan could reply, Seb added, "Besides, Dad would want you to have it more than any other being in this universe. More than he'd want me to take it. He knows you'd look after it better than anyone else."

Logan accepted the gift with a nod and didn't try to deny Seb's assessment. "Thank you. I'll make sure I take good care of it."

"Anything's got to be better than what I'd do with it."

Just to look at Reyes' face wound Seb's back tight and he went for her again. "Not that I'd need to replace your car if she hadn't showed up with that ridiculous mech."

"Moses sent me," Reyes said. "I had to do what he asked of me."

"You *chose* to do what he asked of you."

Although Reyes looked like she wanted to reply, she held her tongue again.

"And you know what?" Seb said. "I'm not even sure I want you in my dad's house. You still need to complete your mission, right?"

A slight pause where Reyes' eyes shifted from Seb to Logan and back again, she said, "Why don't you just go and see him?"

"Do you know what I did?"

"You forced a prison break so you could get away from the Shadow Order's base."

Seb nodded. "You know about our last mission?"

"Carstic?"

"Right. You heard about the parasites?"

"Yep."

"Well, they were created in a gene farm."

Reyes' eyes widened slightly. "You think someone planted them there?"

"They didn't get there on their own. I think *Moses* planted them there."

All the while, Logan watched the pair as if ready to intervene.

Reyes might have shaken her head, but she sounded far from certain when she said, "Moses wouldn't do something like that." It sounded like a question.

"Someone did. If it wasn't Moses, then I'll find out who. If it wasn't Moses, I'm sure the Shadow Order will want to do something about it too. With their fight for *justice* and all that. Although, I don't have the same faith as you do in the big man. I'm struggling to see it as just a coincidence that the Shadow Order profited from the tragedy." Before Reyes could speak, he said, "I'm also going to find out who blew up the shuttle that left Carstic with the mine's only survivors on it."

"Wait, what?"

"There were three survivors. I bet you didn't hear about them, did you?"

The lack of response from Reyes said all it needed to.

"No, I didn't think so. It's not Moses' way to give more information than he needs to. You have to find out for yourself. The survivors were a family. The dad of that family had a theory that the parasites were planted on Carstic as a way to extort credits from the owners. Or to steal the production of ruthane for themselves. The attack happened shortly after the galaxy found out about ruthane and its worth. Now maybe Moses didn't have anything to do with it, but there are too many warning lights flashing when I'm looking at this. If I'm to go back to the Shadow Order's base, I need to know Moses isn't a murderer. I can't work for him otherwise."

"And how will you do that?"

At that moment, the large phone Buster had given Seb

rang. Logan had left it on the coffee table. Seb looked at it for a second, his pulse quickening. He then picked it up. "Hello?"

Buster's reptilian voice hissed through the device. The tinny sound tickled Seb's ear. "We've found out who the supplier of the parasites was. These airwaves aren't safe, so come back to Aloo and I'll give you all the information."

It made sense that he didn't want to reveal himself over the phone. Seb nodded. "Thanks."

The click of Buster hanging up popped through the receiver.

Both Logan and Reyes were staring at Seb when he put the phone down on the sofa again. "I need to go back to Aloo. Buster has the details of where the parasite was created."

Anxiety played out across Reyes' features. Seb sighed. "You can come with me. Once I confirm where the parasites came from, I'll go back to the Shadow Order on my own."

Still frowning, Reyes drew a breath as if she had an objection, but Seb cut her off. "I'm not offering you a choice. You've been following me for this long, you can do it for a few more days."

"I've been *what*?"

"I've felt you following me since I was on Aloo."

"I've not been following you."

"Then how did you know where I was?"

"We heard of your brother's suicide. I'm sorry, by the way."

Seb balled his fists and Reyes looked down at them, adding, "When we heard about that, we thought you might have heard too. We thought maybe we could find you here."

The grief of watching Davey's execution wound so tightly within Seb he felt sick. Before he could respond to Reyes, the voice of his mum came through.

Pick your battles, Seb. She's not trying to antagonise you. Try to see that.

A long inhale, Seb then released a hard breath, his cheeks puffing out with the force of it.

Reyes pulled back as if repelled by the strength of his exhalation.

It helped Seb let go of his rage. He turned to Logan. "Thank you for all your help."

"You're welcome, son."

"Do you have everything you need? Do you have somewhere to stay? I'm not coming back to this house, so it's yours if you want it."

Clearly stunned by Seb's statement, Logan's eyes widened and he looked Seb up and down. "Really?"

"It's a shame for it to go to waste. Like Dad's car, you'll take better care of it than I will. And like his car, he'll be happy to know he's helped you out."

"Thank you." Logan said. "I've always hated my apartment, and I want to retire soon." Before Seb could reply, he added, "There's something I need to tell you. It's about the prophecy."

Something in the old man's kind eyes gave him away and Seb pointed at him. "I thought you knew about it."

Logan walked out of the front room and called back to Seb, "Come with me, son."

CHAPTER 35

Logan led the way to the kitchen, talking over his shoulder as he went. "I promised your dad I'd do this when the time was right."

The anticipation of whatever Logan had to tell him balled nausea in Seb's stomach. His palms turned clammy and his breathing sped up. "What are you talking about? What have you been hiding from me?"

"Well." Clearly nervous, Logan pushed the door to the kitchen open, the hinges creaking in response. "I didn't know if I'd be talking to you or your brother."

Seb deflated at the words. "Oh. So you had to wait for one of us to *die*?"

"I might have lied to you before."

A deep inhale to calm his reply, the dusty room tickled Seb's throat, forcing him to swallow several times. His eyes watered as he gulped against his need to cough. He finally said, "Clearly."

"I mean about checking on your dad's house. I didn't come by to see if it had been broken into." He laughed. "I'm not sure many people would choose to live this far out of the way, even squatters."

Where he'd fixed his gaze on the dried mowgrove fruit in the bowl, Seb then looked out of one of the windows at the expanse of desert. Evening had well and truly settled in, the sky red where the last remnants of Danu's sun disappeared behind the horizon.

"I kept coming back because I knew this day would come. Your dad hoped it wouldn't, but if it did, I promised I'd be ready for it."

"You're talking in riddles, Logan."

Logan walked towards the safe Seb had been aware of for so many years but never questioned what it contained. Several quick taps against the keypad and the small metal door swung open.

Seb gasped to watch Logan gain access to it.

When Logan turned around, he had a small disc in each hand. One had *Mum* written on it, the other one *Dad*. He handed them both to Seb.

Both of the discs had small red buttons in the centre of them. Seb had seen similar devices before. He only had to press the buttons to get them to work, but his thumbs froze as if disobeying his desires. His hands shook and his words caught in his throat. What would the discs show him? Did he even want to know?

At some point, sooner or later, he would press the buttons. Even if he mulled it over for a day or two, he would press them. So why wait? Seb pressed the *Mum* one first.

A three-dimensional recorded image of his mum stood up from the disc. About six inches tall, she wore a long red dress and had her hair tied up in a bun. She looked like she'd gone to a lot of effort to make the recording, and she looked younger than he remembered her, like the recording had been done some time ago. A look up at Logan, Seb saw the man's kind gaze focused on the image, so he looked back down.

"Dear Davey or Seb," his mum said, "I don't know who has this disc, but it breaks my heart to know it's being played. It means only one of you are left. I pray both of you have had long and fulfilling lives."

Tears itched Seb's eyes and threatened to blur his view of his mum. He rubbed them hard so he could see every second of the recording.

"I love both of you boys with everything I have in me. Whatever life choices you've made, know that I'm proud of you and I will always love you. Whatever's happened."

Seb's grief grew claws and raked at his throat. A shake ran through him and he had to set the disc down so he didn't drop it.

The image of Seb's mum sat down on a seat and folded her hands across her lap. "Whichever one of you is watching this, know you have a long and hard journey ahead of you. Your father and I tried to protect you from your fate, but we knew it would be almost impossible, which is why we made these recordings. At some point, everything will catch up with you. I hope you get these messages in time for them to help."

The door creaked and Seb looked across to see Reyes standing there. She wore a sadness all of her own. The footage of his mum must have triggered her own grief. Moses had said she'd lost her dad.

"The main thing I wanted to say is how much I love you. How much your dad and I love you. How we're with you every step of the way as you journey through this life. I hope you feel me watching over you."

"I do," Seb whispered, his voice breaking.

"But what you need to hear now is much better coming

from your father than from me. I love you."

As Seb watched the image of his mum fade away, his heart broke for her death all over again. Tears gushed from his stinging eyes and the lump in his throat damn near choked him. Aware of the other two in the room, he remained fixed on the small disc, pressing the button repeatedly to try to play it again.

When Logan wrapped a long arm around Seb, he fell against the old frant's chest as another wave of grief poured out of him. "They can only play once," Logan said. "What you're about to learn has been set to erase. Your mum and dad figured that if someone finds out your mum has spoken to you, then they'll know your dad has spoken to you too. If they're both gone, there's no evidence. It might protect you for a little longer."

"Protect me from what?" Seb said.

Logan moved the disc marked *Mum* to the side. No more than an empty storage device now. Seb drew a deep and stuttered breath that lifted his chest. He then stared down at the one marked *Dad* still in his hand. After he'd placed it down, he looked first at Logan and then Reyes. They both cried with him.

"I'm sorry," Reyes said. "Do you need me to leave?"

A moment's silence as he thought on it, Seb looked first at Logan and then shook his head. "No. You lost your dad too, right?"

Reyes dropped her gaze.

"Do you want to talk about it?" Logan said to her.

Not aggressive, but clear in her assertion, Reyes stepped away from Logan and shook her head. "Never!"

When both Reyes and Logan looked at him, Seb returned his focus to the disc marked *Dad,* drew yet another deep breath, and pressed the red button.

CHAPTER 36

As much as Seb felt bad for watching his dad's image pop up while he still thought about his mum, it didn't change the fact that unless something else turned up that he knew nothing about, it would be the last time he'd see any new footage of her. At least he had her in his head. Then his dad spoke.

"Son," Seb's dad said, already sounding more human than he had in a long time, "only one of you is left, which is why you're seeing this message. I'm sorry I wasn't there to support you."

A glance at Logan, Seb then shrugged. "Who is this man?"

"Just listen," Logan said.

Seb looked back at the dad he'd never met before. A seemingly kind and compassionate man. "You're the last remaining superhuman in the galaxy. We're actually called Trowks, but we resemble the human race so closely, the term *superhuman* has stuck."

When his dad paused again, Seb looked back at Logan, who knew more than he did at that moment. "Dad?"

Logan nodded.

"*He* was the special one?"

"He did his best to hide it," Logan said. "He didn't want to tell you because—"

"He thought he knew best?" Seb finished for him.

"Sound familiar?"

Before Seb could continue his conversation with Logan, his dad spoke again. "We've lived side by side with humans for centuries. We've hidden our skills because we have such a great power. That kind of power sends people crazy in their desire to acquire or destroy it. I didn't want to give this burden to my boys. But we have one advantage; people might sense we have something about us, but Trowks have been considered extinct for centuries. It's why this message has to vanish after you've watched it."

When his dad looked up, Seb felt almost as if the small person could see him. Like the digital recording from the past interacted with him at that moment. "I'm sorry for how I was, son. I was petrified and felt like the closer I got to you, the closer I got to revealing the truth about your bloodline. I didn't want you to live with the burden I have. Even though I could see you both had the gift, I felt it would be less traumatic for you not to know your destiny. It's been painful to see the disdain you have for me, but please know I was doing what I thought was best for you."

The air left Seb's lungs, taking away his ability to speak.

"The bloodline has been so diluted," Seb's dad went on, "that only a small amount of it remains within you. You can fight and slow down time. But your ancestors … they could move moons. They could manipulate entire star systems."

A weakness threatened to take Seb's legs away from beneath him, so he sat down on the stool by the breakfast bar.

"Davey had other skills to you. He saw the darkness in

people. The policeman he killed wasn't an accident. He didn't choose to see the man's filthy secrets, but when he did, he couldn't cope with someone like that being around. He did the world a favour and kept a lot of child slaves from being taken in by him. But he had to pay the ultimate price to do that. I can see how being in prison—surrounded by degenerates because of the high-security wing they had him in—would have driven him mad. It would drive anyone mad. For that reason, I assume I'm talking to you, Seb."

Seb nodded as if his dad could see him.

"There's a darkness spreading through the galaxy," his dad said. "It's been growing for a long time, spreading out to every planet it can reach. Soon, it will be ready to rise up and take over. You need to make sure you stop it. Find it before it tightens its grip. You need to cut the head off the organisation. Otherwise, the galaxy will fall to chaos. I hate to put this on you, Seb, but the prophecy is bigger than all of us. It says that when I have one child left, they'll be forced to rise to the challenge. Almost as if the death of one of you will trigger *everything.*"

Even being perched on the seat felt like too much at that moment, so Seb gripped the breakfast bar to stop himself falling off.

"Goodbye and good luck, Seb," the image of his dad said. "I'm sorry I was distant. It was the only way I knew to protect you from the truth. Know that I've never stopped loving you."

Once the image of his dad had faded away, leaving just an empty storage disk behind, Seb slid the device across the work surface in Logan's direction.

Logan scooped it up and put it in his pocket with the one Seb's mum had been on. "I need to dispose of these," the old police officer said.

A look at Logan and Reyes, Seb then rested his elbows on the breakfast bar and his head in his hands. "So it's all real? The chosen one, the prophecy, the darkness spreading through the galaxy …"

For most of the time she'd stood there, Reyes had said nothing. She remained silent as Logan said, "Yep."

"I'm not human?"

"No. At least, not entirely human. Your mum was one hundred percent human."

"That's why I can slow down time when I fight? Why I can heal people? Why I can hear …" Seb let his next thought trail away. Maybe he couldn't hear his mum's voice. Sure, he heard someone's voice, but the voice he heard sounded so different from the one on the recording he'd just listened to.

Under the watchful eye of Logan and Reyes, Seb went into himself. He'd left them hanging, but they'd deal with it. *Mum?*

I'm not your mum, Seb.

You're not?

No.

It suddenly made sense. "My god!" Seb said just as he heard the click of the front door opening. Without thinking, he jumped from the stool, barged past Logan and Reyes, and burst through the kitchen door into the hallway beyond.

CHAPTER 37

The second Seb stepped into the hallway, he saw her standing with the front door still open, the wind tossing her long blonde hair. She fixed him with her bioluminescent gaze.

For the next few seconds, they said nothing to one another. Then SA spoke. *I've been following you since you escaped the Shadow Order's base.*

Why didn't you tell me you were there?

I didn't think you'd want me to be. You left without asking us to come.

So why did you follow me?

I was worried about you. I wanted to make sure you were okay.

Seb waited because she sounded like she had more.

Instead of speaking, SA walked up the hallway towards him. Slow steps, she damn near floated with her grace.

Seb had to take steadying breaths to hold onto his heartbeat.

When SA got close, she reached both of her hands out to him. He took them.

For a moment, they stared at one another. The ever confident SA looked to be uncertain of herself. She looked scared. Then she leaned forward.

When their lips touched, Seb breathed in, inhaling every moment of their kiss. Hours could have passed and it still would have ended too soon.

After they'd pulled away from one another, Seb continued to hold SA's hands, his body electric with their connection. *I wanted to tell you I loved you when we were on Carstic.*

I know, she said. *And I wanted to say it back.*

But if you can talk to me through our heads, why have you waited until now?

Guilt and shame sat deep in her azure stare. *I didn't feel ready.*

Why?

Can I tell you another time?

A pang twisted through Seb's chest to hear her say that. To know of the suffering she kept inside. Today had already been too much for him. He nodded. *Of course.*

And please don't tell the others what I can do. I'm not ready for that.

Logan knows.

Will he keep it to himself?

Seb nodded. *I'll ask him to.*

The sound of shuffling feet at the end of the corridor pulled Seb's attention behind him. He looked around to see Logan and Reyes staring at them both.

Because they startled him, Seb nearly let go of SA's hands, but he didn't have to hide it anymore. She knew how he felt and she felt the same way. It didn't matter what anyone else thought. To cover up that SA's voice had pulled him out of the kitchen, Seb said, "I heard the front door open."

Neither Reyes nor Logan replied.

Then to Logan, he said, "Is that everything from my mum and dad?"

Logan nodded. "Yes. You're on your own now, son."

When the tall frant called him *son,* it took him back to the image of his father. After a moment to centre himself, Seb then looked at Reyes before turning back to SA. "We need to get back to Aloo. I need to find out where that parasite came from. Dad says I have to stop the darkness in the galaxy. I don't know where else to start but there."

"I'll get you to the spaceport," Logan said. "Will you be able to get away from there?"

The card Owsk had given Seb remained in his back pocket. He felt its outline through the fabric of his trousers and nodded. "Yes. I think we'll be okay," and then he added, "for now."

CHAPTER 38

S eb knew they'd be there because they'd contacted them from Danu, but when he stepped off the ship they'd hitched a ride on, holding hands with SA while Reyes walked out behind them, his grin stretched all the way across his face to see Sparks and Bruke standing amongst the chaos of Aloo's busy spaceport.

It made Seb's smile broaden to watch Sparks look at their held hands. The slightest rise of one of her eyebrows, a glowing warmth then shone in her eyes before she looked back down at her small computer.

She didn't look surprised, SA said.

Seb squeezed her hand in response. *I think I've always made it obvious how I feel about you. Especially to Sparks.*

SA squeezed his hand back.

The sound of Bruke's excited squeal momentarily silenced the hustle and bustle in his close proximity. Several passers-by looked at him. "What?" he said before charging full tilt at Seb and SA.

SA jumped aside to let Bruke clatter into Seb without

slowing down. It sent both of them flying backwards and flipped Seb's world into slow motion.

Despite being shorter than him, the broad creature weighed easily twice what Seb did. So when they connected with the ground—Seb first—fire ran through his shoulder blades from taking the impact of the fall.

Their clumsiness had scattered a group of jinds, who clicked and whistled their distaste at the pair, but Bruke didn't seem to notice or care. Pure joy as he pulled his head back and looked from one of Seb's eyes to the other. "I've been so worried about you."

Despite the pain in his back, Seb laughed as the heavy lizard creature climbed off him. "You didn't realise you'd be meeting us here?"

"I thought Reyes wanted our help tracking you down. That's what she told us on the radio. Although I had no intention of turning you over to Moses." His eyes narrowed as he looked at Reyes. "Like *she* plans to do."

Another warm smile as he sat up, Seb said, "I know. I've never doubted you, my friend. And don't worry about Reyes; everything's not as it seems." This time Seb looked at Sparks. It took a few seconds for her to look up from her screen. When she did, he nodded at her.

Bruke's head moved so quickly from where he looked between Seb and Sparks that it almost turned into a blur. Then he gasped and pointed a thick accusatory finger at the small Thrystian. "You *knew*?"

Sparks shrugged and returned her attention back to her mini-computer, a frown of concentration crushing her brow.

"Why didn't you tell me?" Bruke said.

Although Sparks looked down, she still answered him. "I wasn't sure you'd be able to keep it in. You can be impulsive sometimes."

As much as Bruke looked like he wanted to take offence, he simply shrugged. He then held a hand towards Seb to help him stand up.

After Seb had gotten to his feet, he watched Bruke stare at Reyes again. "Well done," he finally said. "You had me fooled. Hopefully Moses fell for it too."

"I wouldn't count on that," Seb said. "I can't believe Moses will have sent you two out without some kind of—"

A buzz of electricity sounded out and a fireball lit up in the sky about three metres away from them. A doughnut of black smoke lifted into the air away from the vessel while the charred husk of a spherical metal drone fell to the ground with a *clang.*

Every being in the spaceport seemed to stop what they were doing and looked at the fallen surveillance robot. Sparks addressed the others in a low voice. "I saw it coming and wanted to make sure I got it before it saw us."

"And did you get it early enough?" Seb said.

A look at the beings around them, Sparks raised an eyebrow at Seb. The gathered crowd were now listening to their conversation. The slightest nod, Sparks dropped her tone and stepped close so only he could hear her. "Yes, and I think it's best we get out of here now."

"Good idea," Seb said and led them away from the watchful crowd.

CHAPTER 39

Seb led the group away from the curious crowd and over to the docks. They needed to get the information from Buster and leave Aloo as soon as they could. The longer they stayed, the more chance they had of alerting Moses to their presence—if Reyes hadn't already done that. But he wouldn't let his paranoia get the better of him. She'd given him her word; he had to trust it until he had evidence to the contrary.

Do you think she's told him? SA said as they stepped out of the walkway between the ships, entering the docks.

Can you read my thoughts even when I don't want you to?

I saw the way you were looking at her. I'm worried about the same thing. If Moses was prepared to send a Godzilla of a mech to Danu, what would he send to catch us while we're here? A whole fleet of them?

After he'd looked at SA for a few seconds, Seb said, *Do you think I'm wrong to trust her?*

No. I trust her too. I just think we need to keep our guard raised.

Instead of responding, Seb focused on the chain-link fence with the gate leading to the warehouse. After being on

Danu, the wind coming from Aloo's seas felt like a summer breeze. Despite the taste of salt, it ran a cleansing blast through him, which he pulled deeply into his lungs.

When the group got closer to the fence, the nine-foot-tall mandulu with a gun appeared. It still had lumps and bruises on its face, the swelling around its eye now mustard colour from where he'd started to heal.

A few metres separated them, so Seb raised his voice to be sure the beast heard him. "You look to be on the mend."

But the creature didn't respond to Seb's words. Instead, he looked SA, Sparks, Bruke, and Reyes up and down. "Who are these beings?"

"They're with me."

"That doesn't answer my question. What, you think you're some kind of VIP here? Like you have special privileges? You're one wrong step away from being dropped into the sea."

After rolling his eyes at the others, Seb turned back to the mandulu. "Look, the boss man called me. I have a meeting with him and these are my friends. I understand you're annoyed because I bitch-slapped you, but you need to deal with it and let your ego go. It's preventing you from doing your job."

The broken tusks on the mandulu's face worked up and down as it ground its jaw. A shake of its head, it said, "I can't let you in."

"Are padlocks beyond your IQ level or something?"

Watch it, Seb, SA said to him. *We don't have many other options than this.*

Seb pressed his lips tightly shut. She had a point. He smiled at the mandulu. An awkward few seconds passed before the brute shot air through his nose and walked away from the gate, back towards the warehouse.

It only took a few minutes for the mandulu to return. If he'd had a tail, it would have been between his legs at that moment. Whatever Buster had said to him, it worked. The creature stared at the ground while it undid the gate. The entire fence rattled with its aggressive actions. It then pulled the gate wide, stepped aside, and continued to avoid eye contact.

Seb led the way through the opening and patted the beast on the shoulder on his way past. The creature let out a low grumble of a growl. Such a brute, the deep bass note of his displeasure rolled like an industrial generator.

The last two times Seb had visited the warehouse, he'd come around the corner to find Buster wrapping some creature in chains and dropping them into the sea. Tense in anticipation of seeing it again, he relaxed a little to find the space clear. He led the group over to Buster's office.

When Seb knocked on the flimsy door, the entire thing wobbled beneath his hard contact.

"Come in."

Seb entered first and his crew followed him. He handed back the phone Buster had given him and dipped a nod at the lizard creature. "Thank you."

"You haven't heard what I have to say yet." For a moment, Buster looked at the rest of them, frowning hostility in their direction.

While Buster checked them out, Seb looked at the metal frame. Still covered with a blanket, he didn't need to see it again to know what it represented. The first time he'd been compromised in a while, Buster had well and truly gotten the better of him. A reminder that he could do it again if he needed to.

Buster then threw the dead grub through the air and Seb caught the hard little thing. "The gene farm's on Earth."

"Earth?" Seb said and looked at the others with him. "I thought Earth had been uninhabitable for decades now?"

Mistrust shone from Buster's yellow eyes as he looked at Seb's party again. "Not anymore."

"Earth's forever away."

Raised eyebrows showed that Buster wanted to say it wasn't his problem. He kept it in.

"How do the gene farms even work?" Reyes said.

Buster's brow crushed down again as he looked from Reyes to Seb. He clearly didn't want to talk to her, so Seb asked it instead, "How do the gene farms work?"

"They create creatures that can be used in warfare."

The others moved in closer to listen, but Seb continued the conversation. "So we're about to go into a complex full of weaponised beings marching to the beat of their creator's drum? A complex that's bloody light years away."

"Yep. From what I can ascertain, these grubs—like many of the created beings—are made and licensed to just one person. They probably created one queen, which they dropped on Carstic and let the rest of them move out and multiply."

Not really sure where Buster was going, Seb stared at him.

"What I'm trying to say is you won't have to face these parasites again, because they've probably all been killed since you killed their queen. And—"

"They should be easy to trace because one person bought the licence for them," Bruke said.

Everyone in the dingy office turned to look at the large scaled creature. Buster broke the silence. "Not necessarily *easy,* but very possible."

"Okay." This time Seb turned to the others and spoke to

them instead of Buster. "So we need to head to Earth and find this gene farm."

When Buster spoke, Seb spun back around to face him. "It's in one of the major cities. The place is called London and it's on an island called the United Kingdom. The farm's huge, so when you get close, you should see it from the air quite easily."

A nod, Seb said, "Thank you. That gives us somewhere to start."

Now we need to work out how to get there, SA said.

A look into the calm gaze of his love, Seb nodded and voiced it for her. "Now we just need to know how to get there. Very few ships in the spaceport will go to Earth."

"I can get us there," Reyes said.

Clearly not the only one who didn't trust her, Seb watched Sparks look Reyes up and down as she spat one word. It sounded more like an accusation than a question. "How?"

"I can get a ship from the Shadow Order's base."

"Won't Moses know you've helped us?" Sparks said.

"Only if I bump into him, which won't happen. I have clearance to fly anything I want off that base. I can get in and out before he has any idea I've been there."

At only three feet and six inches tall, Sparks still looked like she could—and would—tear Reyes' head off. Were Seb a betting man, he would have gone all in on the small Thryst-ian. "We're trusting you," Sparks said.

Reyes nodded. "I know. And you can."

It didn't seem enough for Sparks, who clenched her fists and pulled her shoulders back. Seb moved in between them and faced Sparks as he grabbed the tops of her arms. While holding her in a tight grip, he said, "We *need* to trust her. It's going to be so much easier to take a Shadow Order ship than try to hitch a lift to Earth. Nothing flies there from here."

A sharp twist, Sparks freed herself from Seb's grip and looked at Reyes again. "What about trackers on the ship?"

"I'll make sure I leave them behind. You can check the ship when I get back with it."

"Oh, I will. Don't you worry." Sparks then pulled out a small round disc much like the ones Seb had seen footage of his mum and dad on. He tried to ignore the rising sadness it triggered in him.

Reyes stared at the device. "What's that?"

"A tracking device. You'll want to find us when you come back, won't you? Press the red button on this when you're near and it'll project a small local map so you can find us. It won't work at the Shadow Order base, only when you're close to us."

Reyes didn't respond. Instead, she took the device, looked at Seb, dipped him a sharp nod, and then walked out of the office.

After she'd left, Bruke said, "So what do we do now?"

Although Seb saw Buster would have let them stay, they couldn't bring that kind of trouble to his door. "We go and find somewhere to hide and wait for Reyes to come back."

"*If* she comes back," Sparks said.

As much as Seb wanted to say she would, he couldn't be certain. He could only hope for the best.

CHAPTER 40

Because he wanted to distance their group from Buster so as not to bring any more trouble to the slaver's flimsy door, Seb waited until they'd entered the spaceport proper before he pulled the other three close to him. "Reyes said she won't be long," he said. "So what do we do while we wait?"

Other than a cynical glare from the cynical Sparks, Seb got no response. He watched the small Thrystian remove her mini-computer and plug some headphones into it. She then placed one of the ear buds into her right ear and let the other one hang down.

When Sparks looked at Seb again, he said, "That thing you gave Reyes …"

A blank expression, she fixed him with her purple gaze while waiting for him to finish.

"… was so you can track her, right?"

"Of course. But she's not stupid; she'll work that out. And you know what? If she has nothing to hide, then she won't care either."

"Said every fascist state ever …"

When Sparks glared at him, Seb shrugged. As much as he

didn't like the idea of total surveillance, it certainly served a purpose.

While Seb had talked to Sparks, he'd noticed Bruke throwing glances at the crowd surrounding them. "They're looking at us, Seb."

In a voice quiet enough for no one else to hear, Seb said, "Of course. When I was here last, I'm not sure every being knew Moses wanted me. They stared at me because I'm human, but now I can feel the tension has wound up another notch. I'd be more surprised to find a being that doesn't know about the bounty on my head now. We need to find somewhere to hide while we wait for Reyes."

Bruke's face became a wreck of worry lines, SA stood as her usual serene self, and Sparks had slipped her other ear bud in, her attention totally fixed on her screen as she continued to spy on Reyes.

The lack of responses allowed the sound of the crowd around them to come through to Seb. The busy hum of chatter made it hard to pick out the details of the multiple conversations, but he did hear one word repeated several times. *Moses.*

"So where shall we go?" Bruke said.

SA stared at Seb. *You're going to say the sewers, aren't you?*

She knew him too well. *Where else can we go? It's getting tense out here, and I can't think of anywhere better.*

I'm not sure. I just hate it down there.

When have you been down there?

SA raised her eyebrows and tilted her head to one side.

Of course. That was you following me. I still struggle to associate what I saw as a threat as being you.

I just wanted to make sure you were okay.

I nearly killed myself running away from you.

I'm sorry. My intentions were only ever good.

Seb never doubted that. Because they'd had a conversation the others couldn't hear, Seb looked at Bruke to see confusion crushing his features, which he then vocalised. "Well? Are you going to answer me?"

Hard not to smile. After all, he had a way to speak to his love that no one else shared. The secrecy of it made it somehow more special. Something they could partake of on their own. But if he wanted to keep it a secret, or if SA wanted him to keep it a secret, he needed to say something. "Sorry, Bruke." No point in apologising to Sparks, she seemed too dialed in to her headphones to notice much else. "I think we should go to the sewers."

"*Really?*" Bruke said.

A large creature bumped into Seb at that moment, nudging him in the back and sending him crashing into Sparks, who nearly dropped her device.

Sparks looked up at Seb and tutted as she scowled at him. Then she saw the back of the beast as it walked off into the crowd. Taller than Seb and twice as wide as Bruke, if not more, it had skin like an elephant and a lazy gait.

The creature had definitely meant to crash into Seb. He balled his fists to watch it walk away. The edges of his world blurred as his gift threatened to switch on.

Leave it, Seb. SA laid a gentle hand on Seb's back. *You kick off here and Moses will find us in a heartbeat. For some reason, no being wants to claim the bounty yet. Don't give them an excuse.*

When Seb turned back to Sparks and Bruke, he said, "The sewers are the only place we can go where there won't be hundreds of beings deciding if they should claim the bounty on me. We won't have to go down there for long, but I think it's our best option. Sparks, how's Reyes getting on?"

The way Sparks shifted her body showed Seb she'd heard him. A slight lifting of her head, but not enough to take her focus away from her headphones. A few more seconds passed as she listened in. Then she looked up. "She's just got into the Shadow Order's base."

"That's good. Hopefully she won't have any problems while she's there." Now they'd been there for a few minutes, quite a crowd had gathered. As of yet, none of them seemed to want to follow the beast who'd just nudged him. But they had to get out of there before they grew braver. The courage of a mob went well beyond the sum of its parts. It didn't matter how good the four of them were as a unit, they couldn't fight everyone. One quick look at the other three, Seb said, "Does anyone have any objections to the sewers?"

Just before Bruke could speak, Seb quickly added, "And a better idea if they do because we need to move now."

Bruke closed his mouth.

When SA grabbed Seb's arm, he looked first at her and then in the direction she pointed. They didn't have a uniform, but they didn't need to. Seb recognised them from a mile away. Something about the way they held themselves. "Shadow Order guards. And the worst kind."

"*Rookies*," Bruke said.

"Jumped-up little pricks. So damn eager to please." As Seb looked along the line of them, which stretched at least twenty wide, he said, "And far too many of the bastards for us to fight."

At that moment, one of them looked up and Seb's entire body sank. Not hard to find the human when everything in the crowd focused on him. "Damn."

The guard pointed at Seb and yelled something he couldn't quite make out. Not that he needed to hear the words to get his intention. "Come on!" he said, his voice raised as adrenaline lit the touch paper inside him. He ran at the nearby crowd, shoving several of them aside on his way through. The others followed him when he darted beneath a large ship to the shops and alleyways beyond it. From the sound of the footsteps behind them, the guards had given chase.

CHAPTER 41

Seb focused on an alley running between two shops in front of him. The same alley he'd ducked down when he'd had SA on his tail the last time he'd visited Aloo. If only he'd known then what he knew now. Everything would have been easier had he had her company from the beginning.

When he got to the entrance, Seb stood aside and looked back at his friends. SA, as always, moved like a gazelle—graceful, fast, and utterly calm as if she could run forever. Sparks' little legs pumped, and for someone of her size, she had no right moving as fast as she did. Bruke had a wide frame to shift, so he took up the rear.

As SA got close, Seb called loud enough for her and Sparks to hear. "See you on the other side. I'm going to wait for Bruke."

Before Bruke could get to him, Seb saw the first few of the Shadow Order guards emerge from beneath the large ship they'd ducked under. A mismatch of creatures, some ran on all fours, but most were bipedal. Some were taller than Seb and wider than Bruke, others smaller than Sparks. He recognised many of the faces but knew none of them by name.

By the time Bruke ran into the alley, Seb got a measure of exactly what chased them. Like he'd seen in the spaceport, there were about twenty in the pack. They all had blasters, but none of them had drawn them yet. Nobody needed to die today, but Seb needed to come up with a better plan than run. Especially as he'd told SA and Sparks to keep going. But climbing into the sewers might not work with so many guards on their tail. They wouldn't have the time to get out of sight.

The sound of his own exhausted breaths came back at Seb as he tore up the alley. They accompanied the slam of Bruke's clumsy steps and, ahead of them, SA and Sparks' escape.

Although the twisting alleyway stood between them and their pursuers, Seb could hear the creatures behind them. And because he moved at Bruke's pace, they were catching up. Taking a deep breath, he shouted ahead, his voice echoing through the alley. "Sparks, I need you to do something to slow them down."

She didn't reply, but Seb heard the pip of what sounded like an explosive being armed. He didn't need to know any more than that. "Pick up the pace, Bruke."

Everything still moved in real time for Seb. No advantage to slowing things down. It made it easier to communicate with his team at normal speed. Especially with them running like they were.

Several more sharp turns through the alleyway, Seb watched Bruke take each one, pushing off the walls to cope with the sudden shifts in direction.

They rounded another corner and Seb saw it. A small disc had been stuck against the brickwork. A red light pulsed in time with a pipping sound, the pips getting closer together.

A second after Bruke and Seb had passed the device, the pips turned into a continuous beep.

The thunder of footsteps following them through the alley stopped. A cry of "Explosive!" sounded out.

The air dragged on Seb's back, but not enough to slow his progress. It suddenly changed direction, shoving him forwards into Bruke, making him trip and take down his friend in the process. Both of them fell forward out of the alley on the other side as a blast of fire ran over their heads. It burned itself out as a churning mass above them, the heat lifting sweat on Seb's skin.

For the next few seconds, Seb remained on top of his friend, panting from the run and touching the back of his head to see if he still had all of his hair. He then turned to look at the alley to see the walls had collapsed, the bricks blocking the path of anything on their tail. Sparks and SA were getting to their feet about ten metres ahead of them.

"It won't take them long to get through that," Seb said as he stood up and groaned, his body aching from the fall. He helped Bruke up. "Come on, let's get the hell out of here."

CHAPTER 42

A large expanse of open ground lay between the exit to the alley and Aloo's fighting pit. SA and Sparks had opened up a good lead. Seb gave chase with Bruke close behind him.

It looked like SA was headed for the arena. Before Seb could say anything to her, another explosion sounded out behind them. A look back and he saw the Shadow Order guards had blown their way through the blockage. They couldn't go into the pit now. They'd trap them in there like they'd done to the guards on Carstic.

With SA so close to the pit, Seb called through to her, *Keep going. Don't go in there.*

Why not?

Look behind.

To watch the bioluminescent stare of his love widen in horror showed Seb all he needed to see. She got exactly why not and ran past the pit's entrance. *Find a way into the sewers that'll give us enough time to get down there without them seeing us.*

Quite a few seconds behind SA and Sparks, Seb and

Bruke finally ran around the pit after them. The sight robbed Seb of his momentum and he ground to a halt. Nothing but choppy dark sea in front of them. "Damn!"

As he stared at the large body of water, the salty wind stinging his skin and leaving the taste of it on his tongue, Seb shook his head. "We're screwed. We should have found a manhole sooner than this." Then he looked at the others. "You guys go. Swim out to sea and you'll be fine."

None of them showed any sign of leaving Seb there. Before he could argue with them, the stampede of a small army rounded the corner.

Seb faced the mismatch of Shadow Order guards and stepped back towards the water. The mist from where the sea broke got thrown against him, swirling around him on the breeze. A cold line of pinpricks, it helped cool him a little after his run.

A deep breath to slow his world down, Seb pulled one of his weapons from his pocket. To see the sword's handle made his frame sink. Wrong weapon. He reached for his blaster but couldn't find it. He must have dropped it.

Seb pressed the button on the handle of his laser sword and the purple blade sprang from the hilt.

What appeared to be the leader of the group—a frant with long arms and a thick jaw—looked at Seb for a second before her top lip raised in mirth. "What's *that*?"

A couple of the others next to her snorted laughs at Seb and his weapon.

Maybe Seb could take them down on his own with the sword, but he'd need to get closer. To do that, he'd have to avoid a barrage of laser fire. Not even he could dodge that many hostiles trying to shoot him.

"Look," the lead guard said to Bruke, SA, and Sparks. "We've been sent to retrieve Seb. We don't want a fight and we don't want to hurt anyone." The smirk of a second ago returned and she looked at Seb's sword. "Besides, it wouldn't be fair for us to pick a fight against someone with a weapon like *that*." The others chuckled again.

A clenched jaw and tight grip on his sword, Seb nearly told them to screw themselves, but Sparks walked past him at that moment, crashing into him on her way through.

The small Thrystian removed her earpiece and put her mini-computer in her back pocket. "You don't need to worry about fighting us," she said. "We're going to hand him over."

A twist of nervous adrenaline ran through Seb's stomach and Bruke said, "Whaaa … ?"

When Sparks turned back and looked at Seb, disgust twisted her small features. "I mean, look at him. He's supposed to be our leader and he pulls out a weapon like *that*. Does he think he's some kind of pirate or something?"

Seb's head spun to be on the receiving end of Sparks' vitriol. More of the Shadow Order guards laughed.

"I dunno about you two," Sparks said to SA and Bruke, "but this clown hardly fills me with the confidence a leader should instill."

As she turned back to the Shadow Order soldiers, Sparks pointed one of her long fingers at them. "I mean, you lot need to watch out. I've heard he has a pack of cocktail sticks in his other pocket, he might throw a few of them your way if his sword doesn't work out."

Over half of the guards were now laughing at Seb. Heat spread through his cheeks. Such a tight clench to his teeth they hurt, he opened his mouth to reply, but SA cut him off.

Don't.

But she's making a fool of me.

Go with it.

What has she said to you?

Go with it.

It helped Seb calm down a little as he continued to watch Sparks. If SA said he could trust her, that was all he needed.

"I don't know if you've heard of the mighty Seb Zodo before." She had the guards in the palm of her hand as she turned and stared straight at Seb. "I'm talking to you, by the way. Because if you have, you're certainly not living up to his legacy."

Nearly every one of the guards had broken into hysterical laughter. They were so preoccupied they probably didn't notice it. Seb did, though. The slightest glance from his small friend up to the sky behind him.

At that moment, Sparks jumped out of the way and Seb threw his sword at the Shadow Order soldiers. They stopped laughing and parted as the blade spun through the middle of them, narrowly avoiding several of them on its twirling trajectory.

A loud *whoosh* then sounded out and a ship appeared as if from nowhere. Seb saw Reyes piloting it through the large front windshield.

As Sparks ran back towards the others, Reyes lit up the ground with a spray of bullets. None of them hit the Shadow Order soldiers, but they forced them back far enough.

When Reyes stopped shooting, she spun her ship around, showing the open back to them as she dropped the vessel low enough for them to climb on.

Although Seb got there first, he waited for Bruke, SA, and Sparks to jump on. The doors closed when he leaped inside. He watched the Shadow Order guards aim their blasters at him. The shots hit the ship after the doors had closed, ineffective against the tough bodywork.

Seb fell into the nearest seat. A look at SA, Bruke, and

then Sparks, he laughed. "As much as I don't want to say this after the roasting I just got; well done, Sparks."

The small Sparks winked at him. "I figured I owed you that after you deserted us."

Then calling up to Reyes, Seb said, "I was worried you might have screwed us over."

"You shouldn't have."

"Yeah, well, I have trust issues."

Reyes didn't reply, so Seb leaned back into the padding of his seat as she flew them away from there. Best to make the most of what would no doubt be a very short window of rest.

CHAPTER 43

"Damn!" Reyes said, the tone in her voice forcing Seb to snap straight in his seat. Not that he'd dozed off, but he'd certainly come close.

A look at SA, Seb quickly found his bearings and called to the front of the ship, "What? What is it?"

When he didn't get an immediate response, Seb stood up and moved up the gangway to find Reyes pointing at a screen. It showed what was happening behind them at that moment.

Seb dashed to the back window. The sight forced him to exhale hard and he shook his head. "Damn! Guys, we've got company."

Although Sparks got to Seb first, she couldn't see out of the back window. "How many?"

If Seb picked her up, she'd see perfectly, but she'd probably swing for him too. A rough count of the ships, he said, "Fifteen. Maybe one or two more." Another quick check. "No. Fifteen exactly."

SA and Bruke were both on their feet, looking at Seb as if awaiting instruction. The ship had two turrets on the back of it, one on either side of the rear exit. It also had a laser on the front. While pointing at the turret on the right, Seb said, "SA, you take that one. I'll take the other rear-facer. Sparks, you need to get on the blaster up front."

"What do you need me to do?" Bruke said.

Already running towards the left of the two rear-facing guns, Seb said, "Be available for anyone who needs your help."

The world in slow motion before him, Seb jumped into the turret's seat and slipped a helmet on. It had comms built into it. "Can you all hear me?"

"Yep," Sparks said.

"Yep," Reyes echoed.

Yes, came SA's sweet and calm tone.

Locked into place, Seb gripped both handles of his turret, pulled in a deep breath, and said, "Right, let's do this."

A line of fifteen ships, they were the Shadow Order's latest fleet. Shaped like arrowheads, all of them were identical. They were sleek, chrome, and looked like they could turn on a speck of space dust. Every one of them could out dogfight the ship they were currently in, although their blasters might not be up to much against Reyes' ship's shields. Either way, Reyes' flying skills would be well and truly put to the test.

When the ships drew closer and opened fire, Seb and SA let rip in response.

"I'd rather it didn't come to this," Seb said, "but they're shooting to take us down." Green blasts flew from their guns. They scored several hits, the arrowheads exploding from the blasts. Not so hard to take a few down with fifteen of them so close together. A shot in the general direction had to hit something.

For the briefest of seconds, Seb paused to watch the pilots

from each of the destroyed ships. A spherical force field surrounded them and they floated in space, unharmed and harmless without their craft. If they were to return to the Shadow Order once they'd investigated the parasite, it would be good to go back knowing no one had died because of them. Moses could always invest in more ships. He had the credits.

The turret continued to shake with Seb's blasts, but as the ships spread out, he found them harder to take down.

Each green blast Seb sent away from him went off like a cannon. A deep *boom* with every powerful shot. The ten remaining ships rushed at them, fearless on account of the force fields that would save their lives. No such protection for Seb and his crew. Although, some of the Shadow Order's ship's red blasts had already hit them and had little success against their force field. But how many shots before they did?

"Guess Moses doesn't care if we live or die now," Seb called out.

Sparks' voice came through next. "Maybe he's decided to cut his losses and be done with us."

Another ship exploded to their right. Another force field filled with a shocked pilot like a fish in a bowl. "Well done, SA," Seb called into his headset. "Six down, nine left."

As the nine rushed in their direction, Reyes flipped the ship on its side, throwing Seb up so he sat highest of them all.

The arrowheads ran dangerously close to them as they passed, and Seb flinched in anticipation of one of them crashing into them. The collision would be as fatal for both of them. The Shadow Order's force fields wouldn't do well because when they were triggered, they blew their ship's broken shells away from them. If they had another ship exploding next to them, the pilot might get taken out by burning shrapnel.

A moment's pause, Seb wiped the sweat from his eyes. The sound of Sparks screamed through the radio. The nine ships were on her side now.

Several explosions, fire and debris in the air, Seb watched three more pilots float past in protective bubbles.

Sparks shouted, "Six to go."

Reyes levelled the ship out, the sharp movement throwing Seb down again and leaving his stomach up where he'd been seconds before. "Get ready," she called. "They're coming back."

But the arrowheads were too fast and neither Seb nor SA hit a single one as the six soared over them. They pelted their ship with red laser fire, but their shield continued to hold.

"We'll get them on the next pass," Seb said as he watched all six arrowheads throw U-turns in the sky. But instead of rushing them again, the six moved closer together. "What are they doing?"

"They're forming," Reyes said.

"They're *what*?"

But before she could answer, the six crafts had pulled into two tight rows of three. They hovered in that formation.

Reyes shouted through the communication system again, "They know their blasts won't take us down on their own."

Although Seb sent a line of shots at the six—the rattle of his turret blurring his vision—they were too far out of their range for him to do any damage.

Instead of firing back, the six all sent a single continuous line of red light from their blasters. It gathered in the same spot in front of them, growing and turning into a glowing ball like a mini sun.

"Oh shit," Reyes said.

Seb fought for breath. "Oh shit, what? What is it?"

But Reyes didn't answer. Instead she shouted, "Hold on!"

The red ball exploded towards them, a beam of laser—as thick as the six ships combined—came straight at them. Seb heard SA's voice a moment before it made contact. Not quite goodbye, but as good as.

I love you.

CHAPTER 44

The brightness of the explosion blinded Seb and he felt the power in their ship fail. The throb of the vessel's great engines dissipated. Silence filled the space.

Seb rubbed his eyes to encourage his sight back and shouted, "Is everyone okay?"

Nothing through his headset. The power had gone.

SA, my love. Are you okay?

I'm fine.

It eased Seb a little to hear her. *Thank god.* His vision slowly returned to see the ship much darker than it had been moments before. *What just happened?*

We lost power.

Now Seb could see, he watched the six ships behind them charge another red blast, ready to shoot them again.

This one will take us down, SA said.

Better to go down with you beside me than alone. The blast grew brighter as it gained charge, swelling into another red orb of destruction.

When it had grown close to the size of the previous shot, the red ball of laser throbbed like it had the last time. The vacuum of space silenced any sound it would have made, but the glow of it dragged Seb in, hypnotised as he watched the swelling silent death.

The red ball exploded with a bright flare and sent another wide bar of laser towards them.

Seb's slow motion gave him time to think. Maybe too much. But instead of screaming panic, he felt calm. For maybe the first time in his life, he felt ready for it if it came. Maybe he almost wanted it. He'd told SA how he felt, and with the prophecy on his shoulders, maybe this would be easier than what he might have to face.

But then the radio crackled through his headset. The lights in his turret came on. The ship hummed and a vibration ran through his seat.

Just before the blast crashed into the back of them, Seb felt the pull of the ship thrusting away from it, his seatbelt snapping taut across his chest.

A millisecond later, the stars in the sky turned into long white lines as they jumped into hyperspace. The red bar of laser fire released by the Shadow Order's ships turned into one long pinprick like all of the others.

The jump always made Seb giddy. Time travel messed with his physiology. "What just happened?" he called through his mic, his head spinning, his words slurred.

"I made them think we were vulnerable so they'd stay back and take another shot at us," Reyes said. "The first shot they fired destroyed our shield and there was no way it would recharge before they shot us again. I tricked them into giving me the time we needed to get out of there."

Seb laughed. "Wow! Well done, Reyes. You can fly us again any time." The sound he then heard through the speakers in his helmet might have been a grumbling of interference, but it sounded much more like a disgruntled

Sparks. Always the best flier in the group, she'd now met her match.

Before Seb could say anything else, the ship suddenly stopped, throwing him against the back of his seat. He heard Bruke scream from where he'd clearly been thrown across the ship, the only one of them not strapped in. Seb called back to him, "You okay, Bruke?"

"He's fine," Reyes said. "He's just landed in the cockpit next to me."

Although Seb heard what she'd said, he didn't reply, his attention now on the planet just below them. Green and blue, it had a tiny moon orbiting it. They'd reached their destination.

CHAPTER 45

All of them had left their cannons and were now gathered around Reyes in the cockpit as they broke through Earth's atmosphere and headed for the ground. Sparks—although still clearly not a fan of her—sat next to Reyes. Seb, SA, and Bruke stood behind her, the ship shaking with the turbulence of coming in to land.

"There it is," Reyes said as she pointed down at what looked like the only building with any functionality in the decimated wasteland.

The gene farm took up most of what Seb could see. A large green rectangular building, it must have been half a mile long and about as wide. It looked like it had been dropped from space and just happened to land where it did. "I suppose it must be much easier to drop a workplace in a wasteland than build it from the ground up. Although, I don't rate the design of the place much."

"Functionality above aesthetic," Reyes said.

A shake of her head, Sparks added, "Heathens." Although she stared at Reyes as she said it.

Seb watched the slightest smile lift the sides of Reyes' mouth and he smiled too.

Where the abandoned city had clearly been ruined by age, plants, vines, and weeds slowly pulling the place apart brick by brick, the gene farm looked to have contributed to the destruction. Easy to see it had been dropped on the place because the area surrounding it still bore the signs of impact from the large structure. It even straddled a wide river, the banks crumbled from where it had crashed down.

Seb scanned the area below. When he saw where Reyes intended to land, he said, "Is it flat enough there?"

Clearly concentrating, Reyes bit down on her bottom lip, the ship shifting and moving from side to side. "It's the best place in this area. Not ideal, but I can't see many other options in the vicinity, and I don't want to have to schlep across the city to get back here."

A look around, Seb shrugged. He couldn't see anywhere either. "The city looks like it was abandoned a long time ago. Have you ever been here before, Reyes?"

She shook her head as she dropped the ship lower. "I heard the air became unbreathable. An overpopulated planet, the human race chewed it up, spat it out, and then left it like proverbial rats. Despite this being the birthplace of my ancestors, I've had no desire to come down here before." She then fell silent, sweat running down her temples as she closed in on the ground.

The vibration of the ship touching down shook through Seb's feet as it made a loud *clang*. He watched Reyes release a long breath and sag in her seat. "Done!"

With the same angry glare as before, Sparks continued to watch Reyes as if waiting for her to turn and look at her. When she didn't, Sparks snorted contempt at her anyway. "I'd have done that better."

After sharing a look with Bruke and then SA, Seb shook his head at the angry little Thrystian's remarks. Because Reyes hadn't bothered to acknowledge her, none of them needed to either. Still, he leaned forward and clipped her around the back of the head, knocking her glasses off. Before she could react, he said to her, "Hey, how's the air out there?"

Although she scowled at him while rubbing the back of her head, Sparks still turned on her computer and tapped the screen. She spoke to him through a clenched jaw. "It says it's breathable. Although, after what you just did, I wouldn't tell you if it wasn't. How about you go out and test it, yeah?"

"Come on, Sparks," Seb said, "Reyes *is* a better pilot than you. By far. You don't need to sour the mood because of that. Besides, no one knows tech like you do. Don't worry, we're not trying to replace you."

Sparks might not have responded, but she did visibly relax at being reminded what she brought to the team.

The back of the ship opened with a *whoosh* and light flooded in. From how the place had looked on their approach, Seb expected it to stink. But as the smell of fresh grass and flowers cleansed the vessel's stale hull, he suddenly realised the city was beyond decomposition. Despite the look of the place, Earth was waking up again. A deep inhale of the clean air and he gasped on his exhale. "Oh my ,,,"

It's beautiful, SA finished for him.

Seb stepped out of the ship first, his view of his mum's home planet opening up before him. His jaw fell loose. The tinted windshield had dulled the beauty of the place. Grass and vines everywhere, flowers sprouting from cracks in rocks. A vibrant and lush green, the wind continued to blow fresher than any he'd ever felt. He closed his eyes as it pushed his hair away from his forehead.

The ruins of the city contained a history Seb might never

know anything about, but at that moment, it felt like he'd never grow tired of looking at it. Of trying to understand it.

What looked like old fountains sat nearby. They were now dry and overflowing with pinks, blues, and yellows from where flowers had made them their beds. A huge stone pillar stood in front of them. It had been snapped off, leaving a jagged edge where the top should have been. At about five metres tall, it looked like it used to stand much taller. What had once been on there? It must have been important to stand over the grand city.

The pillar had a huge square stone platform at its base. Stone creatures sat on each corner of it. They looked like they might have been lions. Hard to tell with all the chips and cracks running through them. Time had taken its bite from them like it had everything else.

A look behind them, Seb saw the remains of what had once been an old building. It had pillars running across the front of it like smaller versions of the broken one surrounded by lions.

Vibrancy and life all around him, Seb reached across to SA, grabbed her hand, and squeezed it. *I feel like I could stay here forever.*

Welcome home, sweetheart.

Before Seb could continue the conversation, a loud roar called across to them from somewhere in the city. Somewhere behind them. It spiked his pulse and his breathing sped up. He looked around but couldn't see anything.

There!

Seb followed where SA pointed to and his stomach flipped. A lion. At least, it had been a lion at some point. He'd seen them in zoos before, and although large and magnificent creatures, they were half the size of the brute running at them. It also had two heads. One looked like a lion, the other looked like a burned and blistered dragon's head. Both heads had wide-open mouths loaded with what looked to be razor-sharp teeth.

CHAPTER 46

The end of Seb's cry to the others dragged out in his mind as his world flipped into slow motion, mid-shout. "Come ooooooooooon." He led the way in the direction of the gene farm, watching where he put his feet on the debris-strewn ground.

Fortunately the mutant creature came from behind them and not between them and the farm. The vast structure stood as an eyesore against what had been a beautifully desolate city. But it now represented sanctuary.

Although Seb led the way, SA quickly overtook him and arrived at the closed farm doors first. By the time he'd caught up with her, fighting to keep his breaths even, she said, *I can't see a way in.*

Seb looked at the large double doors. Other than a slit down the middle, they had nothing. *Neither can I.*

Sparks caught up with the pair next, then Bruke, then finally Reyes.

"You're not very fast," Sparks said to the ex-marine, a sneer of derision on her small face.

"How about we focus on that thing, yeah?" Seb said,

pointing at the lion creature. Still about twenty-five metres away, it was closing down on them fast. While he watched it, he noticed Sparks turn to look at the locked doors. If anyone could get them in there, it would be her.

The creature closed down on them.

Sparks stepped back from the doors and pointed up. "The electric panel's up there."

"You think you can get in if you have access to that?" Reyes said between gasps.

"Does a two-headed lion-dragon thing like humans for breakfast?"

"Huh?"

"*Yes*, dammit. But how can I get up there?"

About twenty metres of crumbling ruins between the group and the creature now. Seb's heart sped, but before he could say anything, he heard Reyes say to Sparks, "Get on my back."

"What? *No!* I'm not some kind of circus monkey."

"I can climb up there. If you get on my back, I can *still* climb up there. You being so *small* and all."

Fifteen metres away.

A slight pause—barely noticeable even with his world slowed down—Seb then listened to Sparks climb onto Reyes' back, grumbling as she did so.

Ten metres between them and the lion. Seb briefly looked away from the creature to see Reyes start to climb the side of the structure. Although she found small cracks and crevices to cling on to, it looked like she moved up it as if her hands and feet stuck to the walls.

Before Seb could do anything about the creature, Bruke yelled, the primal sound lighting Seb's skin with gooseflesh. To see his friend flipping out helped him relax. If only the stocky beast could turn it on at will. It would be wonderful to be able to rely on his talents.

A regular Jekyll and Hyde, when Bruke flipped into beast mode, nothing could stop him. As he charged forwards, Seb jumped aside so he didn't get trampled.

Bruke and the creature met a few metres away and halted in front of one another. Despite dwarfing Bruke, some of the beast's confidence had clearly left it. The aggression of seconds ago had been ever so slightly diluted in the face of Bruke's fury.

The lion then leaped forward and Bruke's yell turned into a roar. It rang louder than anything the mutant creature had managed so far.

The lion stopped again. Even Seb wouldn't want to fight Bruke in his current frame of mind.

Then Bruke went off. A whirling mess of limbs, he charged at the lion, landing several blows, the beast flinching away from each one.

Mesmerised by the spectacle, Seb smiled when SA said, *There's something beautiful about Bruke in this state. Like watching a sadistic ballet.*

Not that they could enjoy it for long. Bruke annihilated the creature, turning both of its noses into a pulpy mess. The lion head turned limp. Another blow and the dragon head did the same. The large body of the beast then fell sideways.

Seb opened his mouth to congratulate Bruke, but the sound of rolling thunder cut him short.

"Oh no," Seb said, looking in the direction the first beast had come from. Seven more of them appeared. No way could Bruke take them all down. When he looked at SA, he saw she'd drawn her gun. Knives didn't have the range. *You think you can get them all?*

No. I'll try, but no.

I'm going to stand beside Bruke. However, before Seb could take off to aid his friend, Sparks called down to him.

"Here, have this."

A look up at Sparks and Reyes, Seb saw they'd paused their climb and Sparks waved her blaster at him. She then tossed it down.

Seb caught the weapon. Semi-automatic like the one he'd taken into Carstic's mines, he pressed it into his shoulder and looked at the creatures down the barrel of it, his left eye closed. He'd fight them hand to hand if he needed to, but if he could battle them from a distance, even better. A wall of sharp and snapping teeth headed their way. Best to be as far from them as possible.

A look at SA to see she stood ready, Seb nodded at her and she nodded back. He then called out, "Get down, Bruke."

The stocky brute faced the approaching pack, shoulders hunched and fists clenched like he'd fight them all. Although, when he heard Seb's call, he dropped to the ground.

The gun kicked in Seb's grip as he squeezed the trigger and sent the pulse of green laser fire into the beasts. SA did the same.

Seven in total, Seb dropped two of them in quick succession. Both times he hit the lion head of the two, and both times the creatures fell, their dragon side biting at the air, but handicapped by their inability to move.

Four shots and four kills, SA kept her blaster pressed into her shoulder when Seb turned to her and said, *I love you.*

She smiled.

The final beast came close to Bruke, who still remained crouched down. Too close for Seb to risk trying to shoot past his friend. "You're on your own for this one," he called out.

Bruke had positioned himself like a frog, lying on his belly. Spread out on the ground, he looked ready to leap.

When the final beast came close, he jumped up, driving a hard uppercut into its dragon head's chin. The crack of its jawbone snapped through the deserted city like an explosion, and the dragon hissed in clear agony.

Yellow mist hung in the air from where Bruke had connected with a boil on the dragon's chin and the beast flew backwards from the force of the blow.

But it got straight back up again. The dragon head limp, the lion still looked ready to give it a go. It leaped at Bruke and Seb's stomach sank to see it knock his friend over, the large monster pinning him to the ground.

Before Seb could do anything, a green blast shot towards the creature and sank straight into the lion's face, covering Bruke in the beast's red blood.

SA stood still with her gun pointing at the now dead monster.

More could come, so Seb ran across to Bruke to help shove the heavy creature off him.

Once they'd got the large and ugly thing free, Seb looked back at the gene farm. The large double doors were now open and Reyes currently climbed back down the side with Sparks on her back.

After he'd shoved the creature free, Seb held his hand down to Bruke. "Come on, let's get out of here."

CHAPTER 47

The foyer of the large and ugly building looked as bland and uninspiring as its exterior. A vast space lit with bright white lights in the high ceiling. They shone so brightly, it took Seb a few seconds to blink the blind spots from his sight. They'd left the doors open behind them, the sun doing very little to temper the fierce glow from above.

A wall in front of them cut off the rest of the complex and had a door nestled in it. The door looked more like a shutter. Made up from horizontal strips, it looked as if it should roll up to open, much like the doorway into Buster's warehouse. The only other feature in the bland space was a pipe running up the right side of them.

The others waited. Apparently Seb should lead the way. He took the first step across the plain and hard floor, his boot heel sending a click across the empty space.

Just before he took his second step, a loud voice cut him short. Authoritative and hostile, it boomed through the room as if from a thousand invisible speakers. "What do you want?"

Although Seb looked around the space, he couldn't see

how they were speaking to them. Plain walls, a plain ceiling, a plain floor. No speakers or cameras anywhere.

The berserker rage had left Bruke, who wrung his hands as he spun on the spot. He must have been looking for the same things as Seb. His blank expression suggested he couldn't see the devices either.

Seb cleared his throat, the sound echoing through the cavernous room. "We need to find out who bought the patent from you for a parasite—"

The tannoy cut him off. "We don't give away confidential information."

The others looked at Seb, who straightened his spine, pulled his shoulders back, and said, "I'm not asking you. We *need* that information." Before the tannoy could respond, he added, "And we intend to take it."

Silence.

Seb took another step towards the shutter door and the others walked with him.

The door then twitched ever so slightly as the slack in it tightened. The shutter then lifted from the ground.

A gap of no more than an inch had opened up when Seb saw something forcing its way through. A silver bug about the size of his hand.

Once the strange creature had crawled free, it leapt into the air, took flight, and headed straight for them.

Frozen for a moment as he tried to assess the thing, Seb flinched when one of SA's blades flew through the air and cut it in two.

The two parts of the now defunct metal bug landed and skidded to a halt at Seb's feet. When he picked one half up, fire ran through his fingertips. "Ow!" He dropped the heavy little thing.

Fresh blood ran from Seb's cuts, and just as he raised his hand to suck the wound, Sparks called out, "Wait!"

Seb froze.

Sparks rushed to him and grabbed his hand. She looked at the cut. "You don't know what those things have on their sharp little bodies. For all we know, you might be about to suck poison into you." She dropped her bag on the floor, rummaged around, and pulled out a small spray pot.

One sharp squirt of the clear liquid and Seb shouted louder this time. "OW!"

"Better for it to sting than swallow poison."

Seb looked back at the small bug when Sparks moved away. It looked like it had been modelled on a locust. "Something that sharp, with those buzzing wings would have torn straight through me. Thanks, SA."

A gentle nod met his appreciation.

As Seb went to step forwards again, a deep bass sound stopped him. His heart skipped when he looked at the darkness beneath the shutter. He might not have seen anything, but it sounded like thousands of the creatures were heading their way. A plague of razor blades, he pulled his world into slow motion and shouted, "We've got incoming."

CHAPTER 48

Before Seb could react, Sparks sped past him and ran at the dark space leading to the humming swarm of metallic locusts. Although he called after her, she either didn't hear him or didn't care. "Sparks, what are you doing?"

As she ran, Sparks raised her mini-computer, and by the time she'd reached the open shutter, the darkness in front of her had turned into a glinting and glistening cloud of chaos ready to burst forth.

A bolt of electricity from Sparks' computer lit the darkness up with a magnesium glare. Every bug glowed, acting as a conductor for their neighbour before they froze and fell to the ground.

More appeared a second later and the ones on the floor looked to be stunned but not defeated. "They're getting back up," Seb shouted.

Another magnesium glare and they all fell again.

As much as Seb wanted to stand beside Sparks, he didn't. She clearly had a plan, that much he could tell, and him getting close might hinder it.

When Sparks removed her right boot, Bruke voiced Seb's —and probably the others'—thoughts. "What's she doing?"

Another crackle and the air turned white again. Electricity ran a dot to dot through the bugs, revealing a glowing swarm. They all fell and hit the floor in a metal showering rush. Sparks lobbed her boot at Reyes, who caught it.

For the briefest of seconds, Reyes frowned at Sparks. Then the small Thrystian pointed at the pipe running up the right wall. It had a tap protruding from it about three metres from the ground. "Smash that off."

Another buzz, another glare of white light, another shower of metal crashed down against the floor. A temporary measure to their growing problem.

Seb gasped to watch Reyes barely slow down when she got to the pipe and climbed it. At the tap quicker than a monkey to coconuts, she held the boot aloft and looked down at Sparks. "Now?"

"Wait." Another white buzz to stun the swarm. "Now."

It only took one swing to send the circular metal tap flying from the pipe. It skittered into the darkness with the locusts and a hiss rushed from the hole Reyes had just made.

Seb watched on, frozen with the other two as Reyes charged towards them. It took for her to shoo them and say, "Get out of here," before he twigged.

They took off, heading for the double doors leading back outside into the ruined city.

Now on board with the plan, Seb looked behind while he ran. The metal swarm stirred again. "Faster!" he called out.

SA made it out first. Bruke and Seb burst out a second later. But when Reyes got to the doors, she stopped and waited inside. Whether she and Sparks liked one another or not, they clearly had an understanding.

Although Sparks opened her mouth to call out, she looked

over, seemed to notice Reyes, and held it in. Instead, she nodded at her and Reyes pressed the controls. The doors started to close.

To see it unfold in slow motion stole the breath from Seb's lungs.

SA, Bruke, and Reyes took off around the side of the gene farm, getting away from the closing doors.

Sparks ran through the foyer towards them at a full sprint, the swarm rising up behind her, the gap in the doors closing.

The hiss of gas delivered a stench similar to the one Seb had smelled on Carstic—the agent added to ruthane.

The gap in the doors closed tighter and Seb had to fight against his urge to dart inside and halt them. Sparks would tell him if she needed his help.

At the last moment, Sparks dived through the vertical split, which had closed so tight, she whacked her knee as she passed the doors. While in midair, she pointed her computer back into the building and sent a blast of electricity where they'd just come from.

A huge suction of air like a giant dragon inhaling. Seb then dived to the side. He watched Sparks make the jump towards him a second later, the vertical slit funnelling out a tall blade of fire into the ruined city.

The doors closed completely. A charred line ran along the ground away from them. A path of flames had shot out about ten metres long. Some of the lion creatures' corpses held onto them, the flickering amber crawling over their fur.

As Sparks lay on the ground, gasping for breath, Reyes said, "My god, you're awesome!"

A hard frown, Sparks looked up at the ex-marine, smiled, then nodded. "I am, aren't I?"

CHAPTER 49

Seb couldn't help but smile when Reyes winked at Sparks, bent over, and said, "Here we go, little monkey. Jump on."

Even Sparks took the dig with the humour Reyes intended. A half smile, she shook her head. "I don't need to. I can't imagine the electrics will work now anyway. I expect the fire just fried everything. We'll have to pry the doors open if we want to get back in."

An old bar from an iron railing lay on the ground by Seb's feet. He picked it up and held it in Bruke's direction.

Still absent of his berserker rage, Bruke simply stared at the bar.

Hard to temper his reaction, Seb said, "My god, Bruke, when will you accept you're the strongest one here? You need to use this bar to pry the doors open so we can get inside."

Only a mild telling off, it seemed to do the trick. Although tentative, Bruke came forwards, took the bar from Seb, and wedged it into the slit where the doors met. Once he'd wiggled the bar into place, he clenched his jaw and growled as he pulled on it, his thick arms bulging with the strain.

It took just seconds before the large doors creaked and moaned. A few more seconds and the gap down the middle widened.

Bruke roared through gritted teeth, his call echoing out across the desolate city. After a few more seconds of straining, he pulled the gap in the doors wide enough for them to slip through. He looked at the others and let go of the pole, seemingly ashamed of his power. The bar hit the ground with a loud *clang* and he stepped aside, his shoulders slumped.

As their leader, Seb had to go in first. On his way past Bruke, he patted him on his broad shoulder. "You have a place on this team. Without your strength, things would be a lot harder."

The praise seemed to lift Bruke's spirits, the hunched and scaled creature straightening his posture and snapping a sharp nod at Seb. "Thank you. My rage scares me sometimes," he said, his eyes tearing up. "I worry I might lose control and hurt someone I care about. I worry how *violent* it makes me."

"Have you ever hurt someone you care about before?"

"No."

"Well, don't worry about it, then. The violence comes out when it's needed. When you need to save yourself and others."

Another sharp nod.

When Seb stepped closer to the doors, the acrid stench of smoke stopped him in his tracks. A stream of black cloud poured through the gap and up into the sky.

While pointing at the doors, Seb said, "We need to wait for a few minutes before we go back in." He held his breath and peered into the swirling darkness. "I don't think anything's on fire, so we just need to give it time to clear out."

After pulling away, his lungs tight from the small amount of smoke he'd inhaled, he looked at the others to see them nod their agreement with him.

Where the place had been illuminated by strip lighting and light paintwork, everything had now been turned black by the fire. The electricity was out, as Sparks had guessed it would be. It sucked away what little light the opening in the huge doors let in.

Despite the devastated environment, the others followed Seb, all of them either covering their noses or coughing from the thick stench.

Because Sparks had a torch on her computer, she nudged past Seb and turned it on. He followed behind her with the others behind him.

Small lumps of metal littered the floor. The burned machines would no doubt be doing damage to the soles of his shoes, but there were too many to avoid. Every step Seb took gave out another crunch as he crushed them like snails on a wet garden path.

The place had been silent before, yet it seemed even quieter now, almost as if it held its breath. Seb's throat dried and his heart raced. It felt like something could spring them at any point. Instead of breaking the silence, he spoke to SA. *Is it me, or is something amiss here?*

Yep. I've got a bad feeling about this. And it's more than what I should feel because of the situation.

You think there's any other way to do this?

The pause lasted for a few seconds before SA simply said, *No.*

The first to walk beneath the shutter, Sparks entered the space where the metal locusts had come from and waved her torch around. Seb stepped in after her, the tunnel much tighter than the foyer had been. A corridor, it stood about two metres high and the same wide.

As much as Seb's instincts told him to stop, he followed Sparks, and the group delved deeper into the tunnel. Sparks' torch had little impact against the pressing darkness. It felt like the void closed in on them. But the walls and ceiling remained about the same distance away. It had to be his mind playing tricks on him.

Whatever feelings Seb had, they needed to keep going so they could find out about the parasite. They needed to know the truth. Besides, if he had to have anyone with him to go on this mission, it would be the team he had around him at that moment. They'd cope with whatever they needed to. He had to trust that.

It took for them to get close to a right-angle bend before Seb even saw it. Sparks' torchlight sank into the black wall in front of them and she slowed down to allow him to catch up with her.

Together, Seb and Sparks rounded the next bend to see the end of the long corridor. About fifty metres away sat a square of light the same size as the tunnel they were in.

Seb took the lead and picked up the pace. The smell of smoke cleared as they got closer to the light. There must have been ventilation somewhere.

When Seb got to about ten metres from the tunnel's exit, he jumped to hear a loud *boom* from behind them. He spun around to see the others frozen to the spot. "What was that?" His voice echoed in the tunnel.

No one answered. Instead, Bruke shoved through from the back and sprinted towards the light at the end. The coward had well and truly returned. Not a bad choice, but he could have told the others to come with him. Seb chased after him and the others ran behind.

Then Seb saw it. The light at the end of the corridor shrank as what looked like a door closed down from the ceiling, threatening to pin them in. It hit him at that moment, so he shouted at Bruke's back. "The sound, do you think it was the shutter at the other end?"

"Yes," Bruke gasped, dipping his head with the effort of his sprint as he closed down on the shutting door.

By the time Bruke reached the door, it had closed halfway, leaving a gap of about a metre to get through. Plenty of space for him, which must have been his intention. But then he stopped, turned his back so he faced his onrushing friends, and hooked his hands out behind him, catching the door's steady but unrelenting downwards momentum. He managed to slow it down.

Seb caught up with him, breathing hard from the sprint. "What are you doing?"

A strained face from the effort, Bruke spoke to Seb through clenched teeth. "Just go through."

"What about you?"

Bruke shouted at Seb. "*Go!*"

So he did. Once Seb had climbed through to the other side, he helped first Sparks, then SA, join him.

Even though Bruke slowed it down, the door was still closing, and Reyes hadn't appeared yet.

The slap of the ex-marine's footsteps drew close. A few seconds later, she slid beneath the door.

Seb jumped out of her way and then called through, "Come on, Bruke. It's your turn now."

"Come back for me when you can."

"*What?*"

Bruke's hands then disappeared and the door slammed

against the floor as if it was spring loaded. The loud *crack* snapped out through the new room they'd entered and Seb felt the vibration of it through the soles of his feet.

Seb banged against the rock-solid door. It would take more than that to get it open. A deep breath, he slowed his world down, but he couldn't see a weak spot. Then he searched for a control panel. "Sparks, can you see a way to get this open again?"

Silence.

"Sparks?" This time Seb turned to her.

She looked pale as she stared at him and shook her head. "The panel must be on the other side. There's nothing we can do for him at the moment."

Silence engulfed the group.

CHAPTER 50

The room beyond the corridor they'd just left Bruke in had similar dimensions to the foyer. Seb spun on the spot to take in the large space. Unlike the foyer, shelves and ledges were attached to the walls at various heights. They seemed to move up in a spiral, getting progressively higher as they wound around the room. They were all empty. The space must have had some use previously. Maybe a training area for some of the farm's more acrobatic projects.

Still in slow motion, Seb looked at the door that separated Bruke from the rest of them. He sighed before pulling his world back to a normal speed. "The only way we can help Bruke now is to get to the heart of this place, find the information we've come for, and find whoever's locked him in. If I have to put a hole in their head to get them to release him, then so be it."

"Good idea," Reyes said, "but how do we get to the heart of this place?"

A good question. Although Seb had looked at the layout of the room, he hadn't yet seen an exit. "I'm not sure."

An expectant Reyes looked at Seb as if he could give her

more of an answer. Both SA and Sparks looked around the room.

Before Seb could say anything else, the sound of rushing water called through the space. Cold dread fell through him as if the water had already soaked him. It came in so quickly, it covered the floor in seconds. His heart quickened as he looked for the source of the noise. Four shelves—about five metres wide each—were attached to the wall on the opposite side of the room. Unlike most of the other shelves, they all sat at the same height, about one metre from the ground. The water ran over them and fell down in sheets as wide as they were. His boots were already soaked.

Fear sent Seb's world back into slow motion. For what good it would do. He ran across the room, water kicking up at his feet. When he got to the shelves, he saw the inch-high slits running just above them. They were the entire width of each platform. They belched the cold rush out into the room.

Seb jumped up onto one of the watery shelves and planted his feet so the hard flow didn't pull them away from beneath him. Sparks shouted at him, "What are you doing?"

"Getting to higher ground, now hurry up and come with me."

The other three ran over to Seb, SA getting to him first.

By the time Sparks had made it across, the water had reached her waist. Reyes ploughed through the flood behind them. She used her hands to cut a path, sending the water splashing away from her.

After she'd helped the other two up, SA climbed onto the ledge.

Now the others had joined him, Seb led the way, the water threatening to clear his feet out with every step. Although he'd already sussed it, he pointed at the shelves running around the room and explained it to the others. "They get progressively higher. I can't swim because of my metal hands, so I'm going to need to make my way up them to get away from the flood. You can follow me if you want to."

The water had already risen to the ledges they were on. Seb jumped to the next shelf and the others followed. All of them crossed the gap with ease.

What do we do when we get to the top? SA asked.

We'll deal with that when we get there. The shelves must be arranged in this way for some reason. I'm hoping there's an exit up there. After that, he ran along the next ledge and jumped the gap.

The next three shelves didn't raise them much higher, but the gaps between them were small, so Seb kept up his pace, jogged along them, and jumped from one to the next, conscious of his damp boots in case he slipped.

By the time they'd made their way back to the wall with the door leading to Bruke in it, the gaps between the shelves had stretched a little wider. Seb's next jump looked like the widest of the lot. It didn't pose much of a challenge for him, but Sparks, and possibly Reyes, would struggle. *Can you throw Sparks across?*

At first, SA simply stared at Seb as if trying to ascertain his seriousness. When she saw he meant it, she nodded. *Why don't we let them swim?*

We can get up there quicker than the water's rising. That extra time at the top might help.

Okay. She'll probably try to electrocute me though.

Don't worry. Just launch her before she has the time to think about it.

As the first after Seb to the gap, SA stood on the edge, waiting for Sparks to catch up with her. She then grabbed her and launched her across.

Thankfully Seb saw it in slow motion, because the flailing

mess of limbs and bitterness would have been hard to catch at a normal speed.

Once Seb set Sparks down, she glared at him, so he patted her on the head and took off again.

Four shelves later, they were close to the top. Although what to do now they were there?

As the other three caught up to him, Seb fought for breath and looked down at the three-quarter-filled room. He still couldn't see any clues as to how to get out of there. Whatever they tried now, they'd have to try it without him. The exit had to be beneath the water level. "I'd hoped I'd see a way out from up here," he said as the other three stared at him.

SA looked around as if searching too. Sparks looked straight at him, ready to tell him exactly what she thought of him, clearly still bitter from being tossed.

But then Reyes said, "Look."

When Seb looked but didn't reply, Reyes removed her blaster and shot the vent she'd pointed at. The metal grate covering it bent and fell, landing in between them on the shelf with a loud *crash*. "What do you see now?"

"A hole," Seb said. "And it's still a good few metres away."

"Oh no," Sparks said, staring back at Reyes. "You're not throwing me up there."

"But you're the smallest and the lightest. If we can get anyone up there, it's you. Besides, you have the skills to shut this place down. You can hack into *anything*."

The compliment clearly stroked Sparks' ego, because she straightened her back a little and conceded Reyes' point with a nod.

When Seb looked down at the water, he saw just a few metres separated the rising level and them. "We don't have much time, Sparks."

After goat stamping against the ledge they stood on, Sparks spat her words out, "Just get on with it, then. You'd best not miss."

Even now, SA's eyes held a calm bioluminescence. She never seemed agitated. *You ready for this?* Seb asked her.

She nodded.

Seb and SA took one of Sparks' feet each, the small Thrystian shaking and wobbling, balancing by pushing down on the tops of their heads.

When she steadied herself, Seb said, "Ready, Sparks?"

"No."

"Good. One. Two …" On three Seb and SA launched Sparks the three metres she needed to travel. Again, slow motion helped him witness it, but it also painfully dragged it out for Seb. They'd have to catch her again if she missed.

Like when SA had thrown her across the gap, Sparks became a mess of flailing limbs, and for a second she looked like she wouldn't catch the ledge. But then, at the last moment, she reached up both of her hands and clamped on.

For a brief spell, she simply hung there as if collecting her thoughts. She then turned to look down at the others, half smiling. "Wish me luck."

Seb clenched his fist and banged it against his chest twice. SA pressed her hands together as if praying. Reyes called out, "Good luck."

A moment's pause, Sparks then vanished into the ventilation system.

"What do we do now?" Reyes said.

The water had risen. A shake ran through Seb to look at it. So clear he could see all the way to the bottom. All the way to where he'd fall if their situation didn't change very soon. Then he saw movement in the water. A door opened where they couldn't find one before. "What the …?"

Both Reyes and SA peered down too.

Reyes gasped. "Are those …"

"Sharks?" Seb said.

"Yeah."

At least four metres long each, Seb let his breath out in a long sigh as he stared down at them. "They look like it. And they're the biggest damn sharks I've ever seen."

CHAPTER 51

Five sharks appeared. Something so large shouldn't exist. To look at their all too familiar silhouettes gliding along with the laziest flicks of their tails turned Seb's blood cold. Such power. Such dominance. So comfortable in an environment where he was now so weak. On top of that, the water continued to rise.

As if mocking Seb's situation, the sharks cast shadows even larger than themselves on the floor, the bright lighting working against him yet again. "I suppose if you're into creating genetic mutations for weapons," he said, "a shark but bigger makes sense."

"What are we going to do?" Reyes said, keeping her eyes on the beasts below.

Only about one metre left before the platform they stood on became completely submerged, Seb shook his head. "We have to do something before we lose what little advantage we have. As soon as we're in the water with those *things*, we're screwed."

One of the beasts had vanished from Seb's sight. "Where is it?" he said, more to himself than the others. When he peered over the ledge, he damn near lost control of his bowels to see it rushing up at him. It moved as if it had rocket propulsion.

Just before the creature leapt from the water, Seb's world slowed down. It showed him the white scars that tore jagged lines across its snout. It showed him its black stare.

When it broke through the surface, Seb's attention went straight to its wide mouth. Two rows of vicious teeth ran its large circumference. The thing looked like it could swallow him whole.

Seb froze, but before the creature took him, the glint of something flew from his right side and went straight into the beast's eye. The shark snapped its mouth shut and arched its back. If it could scream, it looked like it would have at that moment.

Seb ducked as the beast flew over him and crashed into the ceiling above. The deep and moist crunch sounded like it snapped its snout on impact.

The shark slammed back down on the shelf. It thrashed around, but Seb managed to get close to it. One of SA's knives protruded from its left eye. He punched the creature on its weakened nose. One, two, three hard punches and he turned it off, the beast falling limp from where he'd beaten it unconscious.

Reyes jumped out of the way as Seb rolled the thing into the water and watched it sink like a rock. Panting from the effort, he looked at SA and nodded. *Thank you.* Then to her and Reyes, he said, "Four more to go."

We need to use one of us as bait. When they jump out of the water, I can throw another knife at it.

A deep breath, Seb's mind worked double time to try to find a better plan. The water continued to rise. They'd be in it with the sharks if they didn't do something. When he said, "Good idea," Reyes frowned at him.

"Sorry," Seb said. "I had half of that conversation in my head. One of us needs to stand in front of the sharks so they jump. SA can throw a knife at them, and I can punch them out. If you stand back—" Seb moved to the edge of the platform, shoving Reyes back towards the wall "—I'll do it."

But Reyes grabbed his arm and tugged on it, taking his place on the lip of the shelf and staring down into the water. Just to watch her precarious position sent a flip through Seb's stomach.

The next beast exploded towards them. It came from a different angle, which made it easier to see. It dragged a rush of water with it. This time, SA threw two knives at it. It snapped around in reaction to the pain before it clattered into the wall behind them and fell against the shelf like the other one had.

Seb rushed forward and threw a flurry of blows against its thick nose. Each strike felt like hitting a wet punching bag and he quickly put the creature out.

Before Seb could push the one he'd killed from the ledge, the next one burst from the water. The same happened: Reyes ducked, SA threw two knives at it, and Seb punched it unconscious again.

In anticipation of yet another one coming out, Seb shoved the two limp ones back into the water as quickly as he could. Were it not for their wet, slightly slimy bodies, he wouldn't have stood a chance of moving them. They weighed more than he'd be able to shift unaided.

To watch them sink with the other one gave Seb the briefest moment of relief before he heard another noise that made his stomach sink.

A cracking sound like thick ice giving way beneath his

feet. A glance at where the shelf met the wall, Seb watched a black crack race along it. "Shit! This shelf won't hold for much longer."

The penultimate shark then burst from the water. A greater threat at that moment than the failing ledge. This time, SA got three knives in it. It landed on the shelf, in clear agony from its wounds.

SA shot it before Seb could get to it. Seb then shoved it into the water, which had now risen to within just centimetres of the ledge.

Just as Seb turned to inspect the crack again, SA's voice rang through his mind. *Reyes,* she called, and he reacted by shoving her away from him.

The final shark hit the wall, teeth first, exactly where she'd been. The impact seemed to shake the entire building.

SA hadn't thrown a knife at it yet. The beast twisted and snapped to get at Seb.

When she caught up, SA threw several knives at it. They stuck into the shark's back, distracting it for a second. Enough time for Seb to get on top of it and punch it out. He tipped it back into the water with the other four.

Seb's heart hammered when he looked for Reyes. It settled to see her treading water next to the shelf. He shrugged at her. "Sorry."

Reyes shrugged back. "Don't be. You just saved my life."

Seb pulled a tight-lipped smile at SA. *She'd* just saved her life.

CHAPTER 52

The water rose and Seb watched it, a shake running through him that he had no control over. Despite the crack between the shelf and the wall—the fixed platform ready to break away at any moment—it looked like the rising water would get them first. "Come on, Sparks," he muttered to himself as he stared at the vent she'd vanished into.

When Seb looked down at the ground, he saw the bodies of the five dead or unconscious sharks. They were at least twenty metres down. A long way for him to sink if the shelf gave way.

Another crack then shook through the ledge. Seb felt the vibration of it in the soles of his boots.

SA stared down at the crack, looked at Seb, and then jumped into the water with Reyes. Hopefully it would help to take her weight off it too.

The water continued to rise, covering the platform entirely and lifting about an inch up Seb's boots. He did his best to keep his breathing level and his heart rate steady. Five minutes, maybe ten at the most, and all of them would be listening to their lungs pop as they drowned in the dingy complex. And what about Bruke? Had the tunnel flooded too? Had he already drowned?

I'll keep you afloat.

To look into the cool calm of his love's eyes tore at Seb's heart. *You can't! You'll drown too. There's no point in both of us checking out. I want you to save yourself. I want you to find out who put those parasites on Carstic.*

But—

You WON'T be able to help me. You've tried once already and we needed Bruke before I could be pulled to shore. He's probably already drowned in the tunnel.

The widening of SA's eyes suggested she hadn't thought about Bruke until that moment. She didn't respond.

Promise me you won't follow me down if this ledge goes?
At that moment another snap cracked through the shelf.

Still nothing.

SA?

Fine. WHATEVER. She spun around in the water, turning her back on him. Not that he could blame her for that. He wouldn't want to watch her drown if he couldn't do anything about it.

The water had risen to Seb's shins.

Another snap through the ledge. Then he felt something else. Almost a rip.

When Seb looked at the crack between the ledge and the wall again, he saw the large stone platform break away, slower than it should on account of the water's resistance. For a moment, it looked like it might even float.

A second later, both Seb and the shelf sank.

CHAPTER 53

Back in slow motion, Seb still sank fast, the drag of the water pulling his hair towards the ceiling as it funnelled up his nose.

The resistance created by the large platform slowed him down enough to give him time to think, but not enough to give him time to act. Another ledge below him, Seb moved to the edge of the one he stood on. He waited until just the right moment before he stepped off.

The next shelf held, his knees taking the shock of his halted progress. Seb looked up and saw SA and Reyes. They were on the surface a good five metres above. He might as well have sunk to the floor for what good it did.

SA stared down at him. *Are you okay?*

No.

SA didn't reply. What could she say? He'd simply stated the truth, and she'd promised she wouldn't follow him down.

Then Seb heard something. A metallic voice coming through what sounded like the tannoy above. But he couldn't hear the words. Not with all the water between him and the speakers. *What's that noise?*

Sparks.

She's on the tannoy?

Yep. You need to hang on, Seb. She's going to drain the place.

Seb's stomach bucked with his desperate need to breathe. His head pounded. *I can't hold on long.*

It looked like SA had already sunk a little bit closer to him. Seb's pulse ran a hard thud through his temples. His eyes stung from the pressure. *Is the water lowering?*

Yes. Just try to hang on. Relax, we're coming down.

Strange sounds rang through Seb's woozy head. Internal pops and clicks as if his innards were breaking apart like weakened seals on a failing submarine. He watched SA and Reyes get closer. Light-headed from the effort, his stomach pulled in against itself.

You're doing so well, darling. Hold on.

SA's legs got to within reaching distance as Seb's world blurred. The water was still too far away. A headache crushed his skull. He just needed to hold on for a few more seconds.

By the time SA's waist drew level with Seb's face, he'd stood on his tiptoes, lifting his mouth and nose to the ceiling. Still not close enough to breathe. Nowhere near close enough.

Her breasts came to his eye level, the air painfully close, but still too far away. Seb's legs buckled. She must have seen him going, because she ducked beneath the water and crouched down on the platform so he could stand on her back.

Wobbly and with very little energy left, Seb dug deep, stood on her, and gasped when he poked his head above the water. The call of his desperation echoed in the space. He saw his own fear mirrored in Reyes' wide-eyed expression as she treaded water and watched him.

After several more greedy gulps, the water already at his

chest, Seb stepped off SA's back and pulled her to her feet. They embraced. He squeezed her like he'd never let her go again. *Thank you. Thank you.*

I didn't do anything.

You kept me going. You did everything. Thank you.

The pair shared a brief kiss before Seb heard the tannoy again.

"It won't be long before I can open up the room."

While looking up, he said, "Thank you, Sparks." It didn't matter that she couldn't hear him.

The water continued to run out of the room and Seb looked at the platforms he'd have to jump across to get down to the ground. *You should let the water take you. It'll be easier than jumping.*

You sure?

Of course. Go on.

A curt nod, SA stepped backwards off the platform and fell with a splash. She treaded water as she sank with its lowering level.

CHAPTER 54

S eb jumped down from one of the last shelves, a splash of
water kicking up from where no more than an inch-high
puddle remained. The door that had let the sharks in remained
open. Sparks strode through it and looked at the three of them
before taking in the soaked room. Everywhere glistened with
damp. A look at the dead sharks, she exhaled so her cheeks
puffed out and said, "It was pretty close, then?"

"You have no idea," Reyes said.

Neither Seb nor SA responded.

"I did my best," Sparks then said.

Although exhausted, a headache crushing his skull, Seb
nodded. "You did. And it was enough to save us. Without
you, we would have been screwed."

Another look at the sharks, Sparks raised her eyebrows.
"You sure about that? Looks like you did all right on your
own."

"I was under water when your voice came through on the
tannoy."

"Oh."

"So, thank you. I owe you big time."

"Maybe pay me back by trusting me enough to invite me with you the next time you go somewhere, yeah?"

She had a point. "Did you find out who commissioned the parasites?"

Sparks winced. "You're not going to like this."

Seb let her continue.

"The Crimson Countess."

"*What?*" Seb's voice bounced off the hard and damp walls. "Not Moses?"

"No."

"Okay, well, we need to get to her. But how the hell will we find her? We know she ain't in her palace anymore."

"I found that out too." Sparks showed Seb her computer screen. "She's living on a large spaceship. I have the coordinates for it."

Another reminder of why he should ask Sparks along next time. "What would we do without you?"

"Drown."

Just the mention of it raised Seb's heart rate. His expression must have shown that.

"Sorry," Sparks said and laughed. "Bad joke."

A shake of his head, Seb forced a smile. "We're alive. That's all that matters. Have you heard from Bruke?"

The widening of Sparks' eyes told Seb everything it needed to. "Shit!" she said. "I was so busy sorting this mess out …" She looked at the tunnel Bruke had been trapped in. The door leading to it had been opened too. It glistened with damp like the room they stood in. "I hope he's okay."

An anxious clench took control of Seb's gut as he looked from the tunnel to the others and back to the tunnel again. "Yeah, me too."

CHAPTER 55

Any thoughts Seb had about himself and his own exhaustion vanished as he stared down the tunnel Bruke had been trapped in. Pessimism threatened to overwhelm him. The tunnel sat so dark, he couldn't see very far into it. Although, better than seeing Bruke's drowned body. None of the others spoke as they ran towards it; the scuff of their feet over the wet floor was the only sound between them.

They headed down the corridor, Sparks lighting the way with her torch. Their collective sounds echoed in the tight space.

When they got to the right-angle bend, they still hadn't come across Bruke. The first around it, Seb let go of a relieved sigh to see the shutter door at the other end. It had been forced open. His voice ran away from him. "He got out."

No need for Sparks' torch, Seb picked up the pace and the others followed.

Even before entering it, Seb smelled the charred foyer. Not as strong as before, but it still stank. When they ran into it, he looked at the cleaner floor from where the water had passed over it.

At the other side of the foyer first, Seb burst out through the gap in the large front doors. The sight before him ground him to a halt.

When SA, Reyes, and Sparks came out after him, Reyes voiced Seb's thoughts. "Oh my."

At least forty of the two-headed lion creatures lay dead on the ground. Obliterated. Some of them had one head torn clean off. Some of them had both. A complete massacre. Seb looked down at one by his feet. It looked like its front legs had been forced apart, a deep tear down its chest that exposed its huge, and very still, heart.

Then Seb saw him. "Bruke! You're okay!"

Like he'd done inside the gene farm, Seb led the charge over to Bruke. He slalomed through the dead bodies of the beasts and the broken and ruined masonry of the city.

When Seb got to Bruke, the scaled creature didn't look up. His attention on his bloody hands, he sat with his entire frame slumped.

Still a few metres away from him, Seb slowed down. "You know, Bruke, when you go berserk, it's because you need to. You won't hurt any of us when you're doing it. You know that, right?"

But Bruke didn't lift his head. While remaining sat on a mossy rock, he watched the ground and spoke in a deep growl. "I'm glad *you* trust it."

"And you should too." Hand outstretched to help his friend up, Seb said, "Imagine if you hadn't cleared these creatures away for us. You've kept all of us from harm yet again. Come on, let's go."

Instead of taking Seb's hand, Bruke got to his feet by himself. His attention still on the ground, he followed Seb's

lead back into the ship Reyes had taken from the Shadow
Order. The footsteps of the others followed them in too.
Bruke might be scared of his gift and what it turned him in to,
but at least he'd survived. He could deal with his fear much
better than he could deal with his death.

CHAPTER 56

The taste of the coffee he'd just drunk lay along Seb's tongue, drying his mouth and throat, but he didn't have it in him to get up at that moment for water. His body leaden from the effort of the past few days, he simply sat there, fantasising about quenching his thirst.

In the back of the ship with Sparks, SA, and Bruke, Seb watched Reyes guide the vessel before he looked back at Bruke. Although not quite recovered from his ordeal, he had spoken a few words since they'd been on the ship.

Seb turned to Sparks and said, "Those beings …"

"Which beings?"

"The ones on the tannoy in the gene farm."

"Yeah."

"What did you do to them?"

The question seemed to pique SA and Bruke's interest too.

"*Nothing*," she said, and before Seb could question that, she added, "Well, not nothing, but I didn't hurt them, I swear."

When the rest of the information didn't come, Seb shrugged. "Then what *did* you do?"

"I cuffed them to a pipe in their control room."

No wonder she seemed sheepish. "And *left* them there?"

"Why do you care about them? They tried to *kill* us."

"We're better than that."

"We kill."

"Only when we have no other choice."

"Anyway," Sparks said. "The cuffs were on a timer. We have a day and a half before they're free. I put food and water nearby so they won't get thirsty or hungry, but they won't be able to move far until sometime tomorrow. And when they do, I crashed their comms, so they'll have to go off planet to contact the Countess. Hopefully we'll be done before that happens."

The caffeine in Seb's blood drove his quickened pulse when he thought about what they were heading into.

"And another thing," Sparks said. "I found out that the Countess is behind a lot of the slavery in the galaxy. She's the main trafficker. So if we take her down, we'll make a big dent in that problem."

Seb nodded at his small friend. "Thank you. And sorry, I should have trusted you wouldn't leave them to starve or die of thirst."

A slight twist of indignation on her small face, Sparks dipped a nod at Seb but didn't reply. No one else spoke either.

Seb watched SA lean back in her seat and stare up at the ceiling. She looked close to drifting off, but he said it anyway. *If we're going against the Countess, don't you think you should tell the others about your gift?*

SA sat up and stared at Seb. *NO. I'm not ready to show them.*

But think what you could have done back there in the

gene farm. You could have spoken to Sparks to let her know we were drowning. She could have spoken back to tell you where she was.

She knew the urgency of the situation. Me in her head wouldn't have helped in any way. In fact, it probably would have stressed her out more.

What about Bruke? We needed to know he was okay.

A normally calm demeanour, SA frowned at Seb. *Just leave it, yeah? Don't make me regret showing you what I can do.*

Although Seb wanted to understand more, he didn't push it. He couldn't lose contact with her now he had it. Reyes then cut their conversation off by calling back to them, "We're here."

All four of them stood up at the same time and made their way to the open cockpit. When Seb saw the Countess' vessel, the edges of his vision blurred, his gift about to kick in because of the threat. At least twenty to thirty times the size of the their own, his mouth fell wide to look at it. "I wonder how many soldiers she has inside that thing?"

"Too many," Bruke said.

Upon nearing the Countess' ship, Reyes turned their engines off. She then flicked another switch.

"What's that?" Sparks said. Any resentment she'd felt for Reyes and her ability to fly had apparently gone. Hard to be bitter when Reyes' skills were so much better than her own.

Reyes looked pleased to be asked and bristled a little when she explained. "It's a magnet. This will pull us close and then attach us to their ship." After she'd pressed another button, she looked at Sparks. "This button frees a mech on the top of this ship. Almost half this vessel is made up from it."

The low ceiling in comparison to the tall ship suddenly

made sense, and when Seb looked up, he saw the others do the same.

"I might not need it," Reyes said, "but I'd rather be prepared than not. Right, you lot, hold on."

Their vessel shuddered as they drew closer to the Countess'. The vibration grew in ferocity until it blurred Seb's vision. A loud *clunk* then shook through the floor as the two metal hulls connected. The shuddering stopped and left an eerie stillness in its wake.

After a deep breath that did little to relax him, Seb broke the tense silence. "Looks like this is it, then."

CHAPTER 57

The way Reyes attached their ship to the Countess' reminded Seb of a leech. A metal tube poked from the bottom of their vessel. It had a ring of saw-like teeth around it, which bit into the hull of the Countess' ship.

A circular window afforded Seb a view down the tube. He saw when they cut through, the dark circle of grey steel giving way to light. "What happens when we disconnect?"

"We can leave the tunnel behind so it seals the hole. If the Countess' army prove to be troublesome, we can take it with us. They'll be too busy fixing it to follow us."

As Seb thought it over, chewing the inside of his mouth, he said, "Hopefully it's the former."

Reyes pressed a button that pulled the window away, and Seb went through the chute first. He landed with a slap against the hard metal floor of what looked to be a hall. They'd bored in through a side wall, so he didn't have far to fall. Although he scanned the area—his eyes stinging from fatigue and trying to penetrate the dark corners—he couldn't see anything.

A glance back up the tube at the others, Seb raised his thumb. "We look good for now."

Sparks came through next, computer in hand as she landed. She already had a map of the Countess' ship on it. As the others came through, she showed it to Seb. "We're not far from her quarters." With one of her long fingers, she traced the route they would need to follow. Just one corridor between them.

Once the other three had slid through the tunnel, Seb let Sparks lead the way and he followed behind her. *SA, can you take the rear? You're the best fighter here. We need to make sure we don't get ambushed.*

She didn't reply to him.

The double doors at the end of the hall were about eight feet tall and six feet wide. When they got there, Seb watched Sparks open them, poke her head out into the corridor, and peer both ways along it. "Looks clear," she said.

Best to double-check, Seb looked out too. They were halfway along the corridor. Single doors ran down either side of it. They looked like they led to smaller rooms. At either end, there were double doors like the ones they were about to step through. He couldn't see any guards or soldiers anywhere. He held his breath as he listened, but couldn't hear anything other than the hum of the ship. "I wonder where everyone is?"

Seb stepped aside to let Sparks pass him. "They're probably in their daily devotional," she said. "I'd imagine somewhere on this ship there's a large room dedicated to worshipping the Countess. Also, we landed on the top level. From the map, I'd say most of the activity is happening below us. Other than through the ship's hull, the only way to get up here is to pass quite a few security checks. We lucked out with where we chose to latch on."

A look at Reyes and Seb saw her raise an eyebrow, but she kept her response to herself. Luck had played very little part in it.

"I'll only consider us lucky if we kill her and all get off this ship alive," Seb said. Nothing ever went well for them, so why would it start happening now of all places.

"I thought we only killed when we had to," Sparks said.

"You think we should let the Countess live?"

Instead of answering him, Sparks moved off down the corridor, leading the way with her computer as their guide.

They'd only walked for about ten seconds before Seb shivered. The cold grey metal space didn't have much insulation, and in just a thin top and trousers, he hadn't dressed for it.

When Sparks reached one of the single doors on the corridor, she stopped, turned back to the others, and pressed a long finger across her lips.

After she'd opened the door and peered into what looked to be a small room, Sparks pulled back out and motioned for Seb to do the same.

Just one guard in the room. It sat in a chair in the middle of the space surrounded by monitors. At least eight feet of pure muscle, the white-skinned beast looked like it could punch through walls … were it not asleep

A deep breath to slow his world down, Seb saw the weak spot on the creature's throat. It helped that it slept with its head lolling back, facing the ceiling, its large mouth opened wide. Before he entered the room, Seb tore a strip free from the bottom of his shirt, exposing his midriff.

Her eyes fixed on Seb's navel, Sparks smirked, looked up at him, and winked. "Are you trying to arouse it or kill it?"

"Neither! If I can tie its head to the chair while gagging it, then we can pin it down and tie the rest of it up. The main thing is to silence it before it can make a fuss."

"Wouldn't it be easier just to kill it?"

"I'd rather not kill anything else."

"Unless you have to …"

"Unless I have to."

Two steps into the room—the piece of fabric stretched between his hands—Seb held his breath and leaned towards the creature. If he punched the thing in the throat, his metal fists would shatter its larynx.

Before he could gag it, the beast opened its red eyes and stared fire at Seb. It inhaled to call out, but Seb cut it short with a chop to its throat.

The creature grabbed its throat, its eyes looking like they could pop from its face as it fought for breath. It made too much noise, so Seb continued with his plan, wrapping the cloth through its mouth as he ran around the back of its seat and pulled.

Seb's arms bulged as he fought to hold the creature in place by its head. He watched its pale face turn red. Sweat beaded its brow and a large vein swelled on its forehead.

Although the beast bucked and thrashed, Seb held on against it.

Three or four long minutes later, Seb sweating almost as much as the brute, he watched the beast finally fall limp in the large chair.

Sparks sidled up next to him and stared down at the dead monster. "I thought we didn't kill."

When Seb looked at her, he suddenly understood why she'd said it. "You killed the beings in the gene farm, didn't you?"

"*No.*"

Seb raised an eyebrow at her.

"They tried to shoot me. It was self-defence. Honestly."

"I trust you."

"Sometimes there's no other option, right?"

A deep sigh, Seb looked at the dead guard. "Right."

Images from all over the ship popped up on the multiple monitors. Every one looked as quiet as the one before it. They watched them for a minute or two before Seb said, "Maybe they're running a skeleton staff. The Countess is minus an army, after all."

"Do you think she's even on here?" Reyes said.

While raising her computer to show the others, Sparks said, "Only one way to find out." She pointed at a room at the end of the corridor just a few metres away from them. "This is where her quarters are. We're going to have to go and see because I can't imagine we'll get a glimpse of the place from in here. If anywhere is free from surveillance, it'll be that room."

CHAPTER 58

They reached the double doors at the end of the corridor without further incident—not that they'd had to travel far.

A look at the card reader next to the doors, Seb watched Sparks walk towards it with her mini-computer. "This is going too well," he said.

A gentle nudge from Reyes. "We can only deal with what's put in front of us. We have the skills to react to whatever we need to. No need to create problems that aren't there."

After several quick taps against the screen of her computer, Sparks turned the red light on the door's lock to green.

Seb winced in anticipation of an alarm, but none came. Maybe they weren't expecting them. And why would they be? The beings who ran the gene farm couldn't have told the Countess they were coming.

The double doors slid open, revealing the large room beyond. A throne sat in the centre of it, much like it did in the

Crimson Palace. It faced the other way. Before Seb stepped in, Reyes grabbed the back of his shirt.

When he turned to her, she said, "I think I should go and get the ship ready. We might need a quick getaway after we've put the Countess down."

Although Seb frowned at Reyes, SA's voice came through to him. *She's right. She wants to stay and fight, but she'll be much more use to us if she's ready to get us out of here.*

After Seb nodded at her, Reyes ran away from them in the direction of the ship. Her steps, although light, certainly weren't soundless in the long and abandoned corridor.

Seb stepped into the large room first. Before he had time to take the place in, the throne spun around to face them. The red robed figure of the Countess sat in it, her dark hood staring straight at them.

Sparks locked the doors behind them and Seb watched SA draw her blades. Bruke then raised a semi-automatic blaster, and now Sparks had secured the doors, she did the same.

In this situation, with only one enemy, Seb chose to leave his gun sheathed in his belt. The cold metal of it pressed against his back. He clenched his fists while stepping forwards. "Normally we don't kill," he said, "but sometimes the justice system isn't equipped for dealing with the kind of crimes *you've* committed."

The Countess' hood twitched as if she was about to speak. But she didn't.

"Slavery, murder, terrorist activities, extortion … you don't deserve to live."

The sound of the group's steps closed down on the Countess, and Seb heard something coming back from her: heavy and laboured breaths.

Just a few metres separating them, the Countess shook her head but still didn't speak.

A sting burned Seb's tired eyes as he continued to watch her without blinking. He moved closer, tense and ready to fight. "It had to happen sooner or later. You can't live a life like yours and not have it come back to bite you on the arse at some point."

An almost asthmatic snort, the Countess' breaths sped up and she shook where she sat. But Seb still couldn't see her face in the darkness of her hood. He stepped closer still, holding his breath. Tension turned the air thick, waiting for the spark.

So close he could smell the rotten stench coming from her, her breaths hot and heavy. His world in slow motion, Seb leaned forwards with a shaking hand, pinched the material on her hood, and threw it backwards to expose her face.

The sight forced him to stumble back a few steps, and although he opened and closed his mouth, he couldn't get his words out.

He finally said, "Gurt?"

CHAPTER 59

The sound of an alarm rang out, the shrill tone of it snapping through Seb and forcing him to jump back another step. Yet he still remained transfixed on his dead friend. How had the Countess brought him back to life?

But then Gurt's face changed, the illusion moving aside to show the true being beneath.

The creature, although about the same size and build as Gurt, had a much smaller head. Almost ape-like, it was vibrant green like a tree snake. It had bruises, cuts, and blood all over its face from where it had clearly been beaten. On the brink of death, it seemed to take a great effort for it to speak. "The Countess wanted to give you a message; she isn't as stupid as you think."

A fireball of an explosion went off inside the creature's head, lighting up its eyes and mouth like a jack-o'-lantern. Seb covered his face with his hands. The backs of them got splattered with hot wet chunks. The heat from the fireball lifted sweat on his skin. When he looked at the others, he saw they were covered in blood and flesh too.

The bright white lights in the room then dimmed and turned red. They pulsed in time with the loud alarm.

SA, Seb said, *you need to show the others what you can do. They won't hear me over this noise.*

No.

Come on, don't be so selfish.

You don't understand.

I understand you're putting us at risk because you want to keep your gift to yourself. If you don't tell them, I will.

Shut up, Seb.

The words stung and halted Seb momentarily. Accompanied by SA's glare, it cut deep. But he had no time for his feelings, especially when a voice came over the tannoy system.

It took a few words for Seb to identify the deep boom as female. "You think we didn't see you coming? I thought you were smarter than to walk straight into a trap."

SA, we need you to help us.

SA didn't even look at him this time.

We'll die if you don't.

Just focus on the fight.

Before Seb could say anything else, he saw that each of the four walls had double doors in them like the ones they'd entered through. Three of them opened. The ones they'd entered via remained closed. A stampede of Crimson soldiers poured into the room. They were all dressed in the crimson robes of their queen, their faces hidden in shadow.

The four Shadow Order members pulled together, their backs facing the still-closed doors as they readied themselves for the oncoming threat.

Sparks let rip first, sending a pulse of laser fire from her automatic blaster. She blew four guards away. More replaced them, jumping over their fallen comrades without breaking stride. It seemed like an impossible fight. There were more guards than the four of them could kill.

As one, the group moved closer to the doors Reyes had exited through. Sparks had locked them, so hopefully they'd stay locked. They needed to avoid being surrounded.

As Sparks continued to fire, Seb said, "Be careful, those guns overheat."

At his call, Sparks let go of the trigger, the blasts dying for a second before she ripped off another line of shots. If she waited too long, they wouldn't last past the first minute of the battle.

A stream of knives flew away from the group quicker than Spark's automatic rifle could send out blasts. It slowed the soldiers down, but they were still making ground on them.

SA, they won't be able to hear my instructions over the alarm. You have to show them what you can do.

They were now just a few metres away from the locked doors. *Drag the soldiers with you over to the other side of the hangar away from us,* SA said. *Get to the far corner.*

You want me to go over there on my own?

Yes. You're the only one that can do it and avoid being shot.

As hard as he found it to trust her at that moment, Seb shouted at the other two, "Follow SA's lead." He shared a look with her before he made a break for it. The Crimson soldiers filled each of the doorways and fought from there. Those at the front knelt down so the ones behind could shoot over them. They sent two lines of blasts at Seb as he ran.

It took all Seb had to avoid the laser fire, the other three taking out the soldiers while they focused on him. *What am I? Target practice or something?*

Just get to the far corner. I'll deal with everything else.

How will you do that if you won't talk to them? I feel like you just want to get me away from them so you can keep your secret safe. You're putting us all at risk here.

SA ignored him, and when he got to the farthest corner away from the others, he turned around to see the soldiers had moved from their positions and were closing in on him. Although the others took some down, the Crimson Soldiers' lives were cheap. They could afford casualties.

What are you doing, SA? Seb said. *You're going to get me killed.*

Shut up and hold your breath.

Is that a joke?

DO IT!

Seb held his breath and looked across the room at SA. She glared at him. He'd clearly crossed a line with her. She then slammed her hand against the control panel by the door behind her.

A second later, a frigid rush of air pulled on Seb's back. It ripped him from his feet and dragged him out of the airlock behind him.

CHAPTER 60

As Seb flew backwards out of the open airlock, a pressure clamped his chest, threatening to crush the air from it. It dared him to breathe, but SA's words rang through his mind. He pressed his lips tightly together. He had to trust her.

Panic accelerated Seb's pulse to see the fear surrounding him. Many of the soldiers being dragged from the airlock had had their hoods ripped back, revealing twisted faces. In a hopeless attempt to do something, he flailed his arms and legs as if he could swim against the force dragging him into oblivion. He couldn't.

The cold of Seb's surroundings ran through his extremities first, needles of pain threatening to destroy any feeling he had in his fingers and toes. Then he crashed—back first—into something hard and metal. He hadn't seen it coming and it damn near winded him. But he fought against his desire to gasp and kept his breath held. The metal object continued forward, taking him back into the ship with it.

When Seb re-entered the ship, he looked across at SA, his vision blurred from where his eyes watered. She was stopping herself from being dragged outside by holding onto a handle near the double doors. She reached out to press a button next to the card reader. The same button she'd pressed to launch him out into oblivion.

After she'd crashed her hand against it, the airlock slammed shut, cutting a Crimson soldier in two. Seb stared at the red bloodstain as the throne room re-pressurised. Only when he had nothing left, Seb finally trusted he could breathe again. He gasped and fell forward, fighting to get his breath back, barking like a seal.

Unable to speak, Seb felt like his lungs had shrunk. But he shouldn't panic. He'd get his breath back; he just needed to calm down. It took a great effort for him to crawl over to the closest wall and lean against it, his body still heaving with his need for air.

Seb watched the mech that had dragged him back in. She faced the crimson soldiers with her two fists stretched out in front of her. They then folded down, revealing two Gatling guns in her wrists. They protruded like they were bones running through her forearms.

Despite how many soldiers they'd flushed out up until that point, a flow of them still ran in through the three sepa-rate doors. The mech's guns whirred as she cleared one of the doorways in seconds. She then turned to the next two and did the same, tearing the soldiers to shreds in a spray of blood and flesh. Being the main aggressor at that moment, she drew the soldiers' fire. The red laser blasts bounced off her seem-ingly impenetrable shell.

The three doors didn't stay cleared for long. The mech returned her focus to the first door and took out the next wave to burst from it.

Yes, you're hearing me, SA said, *but we don't have time for questions.*

It took for Seb to look at Bruke and Sparks, confusion on Sparks' face, fear on Bruke's, to realise SA had addressed everyone. *See,* he said, *I knew you could do it. This is what we need.*

A dark stare at Seb, SA then said, *Sparks and Bruke, you stay here and fight with Reyes and me.* She then threw a knife across the space into a Crimson soldier that looked like it had died. From the way it twitched at the killer shot, it had clearly been acting. *Seb, I can see the Countess getting away.*

A look to where SA pointed, Seb saw the tall figure in a crimson robe. Because they were surrounded by robes and he'd been dragged outside, he'd lost track of which one the Countess was. But now SA had pointed her out and she was running out of there through a separate, smaller door, it seemed so obvious.

Can you get to her if we hold the soldiers back?

You were talking to Reyes all along, weren't you?

SA glared at Seb again. *Can you get to the Countess?*

Yes, I can. I'm sorry, SA; I should have trusted you.

SA looked at Seb like she wanted to knock him out. *Just do your job, yeah?*

As much as Seb wanted to talk to her, wanted to apologise for not trusting her again, now certainly wasn't the time. He pulled another deep breath in as he got to his feet. Just about recovered, he ran in the direction of the Countess and said nothing more.

CHAPTER 61

The burden of SA's scorn weighed heavy on Seb's mind as he ran through the doorway the Countess and several of her guards had just disappeared through. He emerged into a tight corridor. It looked like the one they'd entered the throne room via but smaller; it was also made from gunmetal grey, exposed steel and almost as cold as the space he'd just been dragged out into. As he ran, his breath turned to condensation in front of his face.

Bright lights ran along the corridor's ceiling like they did in most of the ship. The hard space amplified the stampeding footsteps of the escaping Countess and her crew.

Just before the Countess and her guards disappeared around the first bend, Seb counted seven of them in total.

Four guards and the Countess vanished while two guards turned their guns on him. They released a volley of red laser fire. The blasts came in slow motion, and although numerous, they would have been easier to avoid had they not crashed into the walls and floor around him. Every contact shattered the blast into a thousand sparks. It rendered them ineffective, but they hid the shots that came through behind them.

Seb dodged and weaved, zigzagging his way up the tight corridor to avoid the blasts until he came to the first guard. No point in returning fire, he arrived without being shot and saw the weak spot in its chest. He drove the hardest blow he could at it. His fist sank with a crack of sternum and ribs. The creature gasped, expelling rancid breath from its dark hood. The halitosis smell made Seb heave.

The next guard went down with a bone-crunching punch into the centre of its hood.

Despite the contempt he'd just received from her, it lifted Seb to hear SA's voice as he ran. *How are you doing?*

I've taken down two of her six guards. They won't be getting back up again.

Only when necessary, eh?

Exactly.

Seb caught up with the remaining four guards and the Countess. The two guards at the back looked around as if they considered stopping. But then he saw the Countess wave them forward and they all vanished around the next corner.

A few seconds later, Seb came to a room with a long bridge across it. It had a large generator beneath the bridge. It hung as a huge sphere, a globe larger than Reyes' ship. It was suspended in a vast space that dropped so far he couldn't see the bottom. The generator looked to be held in place with a magnetic force. He couldn't see any other reason for it to hang in midair without wires or a structure of any sort.

To look down made Seb's stomach lurch, so he stared across the bridge to the exit and ran for it.

About a quarter of the way along the skinny bridge, Seb saw the Countess and her guards reach the other side. If a shadowed hood could grin, the Countess grinned at him at that moment as she slapped her hand against a button on the wall by the doorway. She then ran off.

The slamming of the door behind Seb came down with an almighty *boom.* A guillotine of a drop, it cut off his retreat. The image of the soldier chopped in half in the airlock came back to him.

The bridge then started to withdraw in front of Seb. It pulled away from the doorway the Countess had just run through. Only a small gap at present, it was growing with every passing second.

Too far to run, the gap would be too large by the time Seb got to it. Not that he had any other choice but to try. While gritting his teeth, he sped up. A useless gesture, but what else could he do?

CHAPTER 62

T he curse of slow motion showed Seb that no matter how fast he ran along the metal bridge, he wouldn't make the jump across the ever-widening gap. He'd not even made it to the halfway point and the gap already looked too large for him to clear. *Goodbye. And sorry I didn't trust you.*

WHAT?

I'm not going to make it out of here.

Where are you?

But before Seb could answer her, something tugged on his hands. The closer he got to the middle of the bridge, the harder the pull. He looked down at the chrome sphere below him. Of course! The force that held the globe in place had to be strong enough to tug on his fists.

No chance of making the jump, he had to try something else.

Seb leaped from the side of the bridge, diving towards the generator with his clenched fists stretched out in front of him. An impossible fall, but the generator's tug seemed strong enough.

It was working, the generator's magnetism dragging him in.

When Seb got close to the sphere, he pulled his hands behind his back to stop his fists sticking to it. It took some effort, his arms aching against the force, but he managed it. It lessened the pull so he fell down rather than at the large metal ball.

Although close enough to touch it, Seb didn't get any closer. Mesmerised by the reflective surface as he rushed past the generator, he had to shake his head to snap out of it. Just before he cleared the bottom of the sphere, he raised his fists up. The magnetic tug worked against his fall and dragged him around the bottom of the large ball.

Seb flew beneath the huge globe, his legs swinging under him in a pendulous arc.

On the upswing, Seb did the same as he had on the way down; he pulled his hands as far away from the magnetic force as he could. He used his momentum to send him up towards the small doorway the Countess and her guards had disappeared through.

Just one chance to make it, Seb focused on the space. The magnetic tug pulled against him, but not hard enough to halt him.

When Seb reached out to catch the doorway, the pull of the generator dragged on his fists, ripping the top half of him backwards.

Seb's feet swung out in front of him and over his head. The back of his heels now led the way. He closed his eyes, pulled his fists into his stomach, and gave himself over to fate.

The base of Seb's back crashed into the wall above the door, his heels hitting the gunmetal grey farther up. A nauseating crack snapped through him. His momentum carried the top half of his body through the doorway, spinning him into the space beyond.

Seb collided, face first, with the metal wall in front of him, hitting it so hard it sent a shockwave through his skeleton and dragged up the metallic taste of his own blood.

When he hit the hard ground in a heap, Seb panted and dared not move. What if he'd broken every bone in his body?

SA's voice came through. It had been there all along, but he could only focus on it now. *Seb? Are you okay?*

Gentle movements, Seb stretched out his limbs and looked around. He'd made it. The sound of his own laugh ran away from him down the corridor. *Yeah, I'm fine.*

After standing up on shaking legs, Seb looked up the hallway. The Countess and her guards had gone. Not sure where to go now, at least he had a chance. *I'll let you know when I find her.*

Woozy from the crash landing, Seb broke into a clumsy run up the tight corridor. After a few strides, he found his bearings, his adrenaline numbing what he could feel would become fierce pain.

CHAPTER 63

The world still in slow motion, Seb had the advantage when he burst into the room they were in because they clearly hadn't expected him. He ran at the four guards and took them down in quick succession. He hit two of them in the face, one in the stomach, and one in the shins. None of them showed any signs of getting back up again.

By the time Seb had spun around to deal with the Countess, he found her pointing a blaster at his face. At least three feet taller than him, viewing her past the barrel of her gun made her seem even bigger.

They stared at one another for what felt like an age, Seb frozen as he peered into the darkness of the Countess' hood.

A flash of laser fire came from the right. Seb watched the Countess release her grip on her blaster, a blacked hole now in the back of her hand. She screamed with a force that rattled through his skull and blew his hair back.

Before the Countess could do anything else, Seb punched her in the throat. If for no other reason than to silence the scream. He showed a little restraint, hitting her just hard enough to knock her down, but not so hard that he broke her neck. They needed her alive. They needed answers.

The Countess fell so hard to the ground it seemed to shake the entire ship. Seb looked up at SA, Bruke, Reyes, and Sparks. Bruke kept his gun raised from where he'd shot her. He then looked back at the large hooded figure on the floor. "Shall I pull her hood back?"

None of them answered. Instead, they all stared at her as if awaiting his decision.

CHAPTER 64

The group had waited for another few minutes in silence before Seb had finally been the one to pull the Countess' hood back. Both Reyes and Bruke vomited instantly, so he covered it over again.

To think about it as they flew away in Reyes' ship left him confused. He couldn't pick out what it was about her burned and blackened face that bothered him so much. Sure, it looked revolting. Her lips were scorched away, so her teeth were permanently displayed. But something about seeing it gave him a feeling he'd not experienced before. Almost as if the vision of her had a dark force that reached inside him, grabbed his guts, and squeezed hard.

Also, for some reason, when he'd seen her, he'd nearly lost control of his bowels and a noise went off in his head like a thousand tortured souls cried out to him. Maddening and indecipherable, it sounded like it could have been the echoes of all the slaves she'd tortured. It seemed like everything about her paid a karmic debt for the life she'd chosen. Maybe the others had felt it too because no one had spoken since.

They were heading back to Aloo. The Countess lay alive

but unconscious at their feet. She wouldn't get a fair trial; she didn't deserve it. But she had answers to questions they needed to ask her.

SA then came through Seb's thoughts.

I've always been able to communicate telepathically. I chose not to for the longest time, and for that I'm sorry. She glared at Seb. *Although I have good reasons, despite what Seb thought.* The others then looked at him too.

My family were slaughtered when I was a kid. To look at this evil bitch, knowing what she's done, reminds me of that time. I was young, too young. I was taken in by the monastery in our village. They practiced martial arts all day every day and never spoke.

I learned early on that I could communicate with telepathy, but never used the gift. As a monk, we should always listen and never voice our own thoughts. They're not that important. But then one day, I said something in my mind to another monk. It just slipped out. I couldn't help it.

A sheen of tears spread across SA's eyes, glazing them and magnifying their bioluminescence.

"What happened?" Bruke asked.

They kicked me out of the monastery. They called me a freak and said my desire to disobey their rules was so strong it had turned me into a witch. I was TWELVE years old. I had to survive on my own after that. Fortunately, I'd been trained to fight. I could look after myself. Seb was the first person I've shown my gift to since then. I was worried I'd be rejected again.

To hear her story hurt Seb's heart. "I'm so sorry I pushed you to speak to the others. I thought we needed it."

You often think you know best.

The expression on the faces of the others showed Seb she was speaking only to him. Before he could reply, she spoke again, not angry, just sad. *And that's the problem, isn't it? No matter how far forward we step, you always try to make decisions for me. Decisions like your dad made for you.*

Although Seb wanted to reply, SA spoke to the others again. *I was talking to Reyes in the mech when we got trapped by the Countess and her army. I knew the airlock would work if we could get her there. I didn't have the headspace to talk to you guys and direct her. Also, I wanted the mech to be a surprise. If none of you knew, there would be less chance of someone giving the game away to the Countess. I gambled everything on it working.*

Again she switched to just Seb. *I'm not sure we can work if you never trust me.*

I do.

SA didn't reply. After a deep breath, she looked at Seb again. The hurt had lifted a little. *I suppose in some way it was sweet of you.*

Huh?

Well, I felt like a freak for what I could do, but that didn't even enter your mind. That's why you couldn't understand why I didn't use my gift. That was sweet. In a strange and frustrating way, it showed me you accept me for who I am.

I do. Of course I do.

Seb stepped towards SA. He was about to grab her hands, but the Countess stirred next to them.

Even groggier than before, the Countess' voice bubbled from her throat when she turned to Seb. "How did you manage to follow me?"

"That's a good point." Seb looked at Sparks. "I meant to ask you the same. Did you hack the bridge so it stretched back across?"

A curt nod, she looked almost offended by the question. "Of course. It wasn't hard."

Although he hadn't answered the Countess, Seb said, "Why did you put the parasite on Carstic?"

"Ruthane, why else?"

"Just for the credits?"

"Yeah. What other reason is there to act in this galaxy?"

She sounded like Moses. "And the shuttle?"

"The one to leave the planet?"

"Yep."

"That was me. The pilot was working for me, but when I heard someone was coming off Carstic looking to throw accusations about how the parasite got there, I couldn't let them live."

A slight pause, Seb froze. "How did you get that information about who was on the flight? That was a private conversation between Moses and myself."

The Countess' laugh rang around the small ship. "Oh, you're such a fool. You still haven't worked it out yet, have you?"

A look at the others, Seb returned his focus to the bound Countess. "Worked what out?"

"Moses was in on it. Who do you think gets paid when something like the parasites invade a planet?"

A moment of stillness as Seb tried to control his rage. He'd known Moses was in on it all along. He should have acted on his hunch weeks ago. The horrible shark didn't deserve to live.

"Naive little fool," the Countess said and laughed again.

Seb pulled his gun from his belt and ripped a shot off into her hood. The reek of cauterised flesh smoked from the shadowy hole and she snapped limp.

The others stared at Seb, their faces slack.

"Some beings don't deserve to live," he said. "I gave her longer than I wanted to anyway. We need to send her out the airlock so she can float in the void of space. That's all she's earned from this life."

"So what do we do now?" Sparks said.

A steadying breath to try to bring his fury down, Seb clenched his jaw. "We go to Aloo. It's time Moses paid for the way he conducts his business."

END OF BOOK FIVE.

∽

Thank you for reading Fugitive - Book Five of The Shadow Order.

∽

Want more of the Shadow Order, and specifically Reyes? Dive into a story set in her past and get to know her better in 120-Seconds: A Shadow Order Story - available at www.michaelrobertson.co.uk

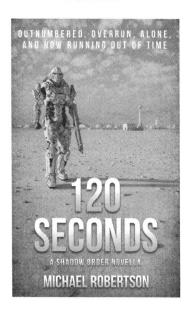

Support the Author

DEAR READER, AS AN INDEPENDENT AUTHOR I DON'T HAVE the resources of a huge publisher. If you like my work and would like to see more from me in the future, there are two things you can do to help: leaving a review, and a word-of-mouth referral.

RELEASING A BOOK TAKES MANY HOURS AND HUNDREDS OF dollars. I love to write, and would love to continue to do so. All I ask is that you leave an Amazon review. It shows other readers that you've enjoyed the book and will encourage them to give it a try too. The review can be just one sentence, or as long as you like.

Would you like to be notified of all of my updates and special offers? Join my mailing list at www. michaelrobertson.co.uk

If you've enjoyed The Shadow Order, you may also enjoy my post-apocalyptic series - The Alpha Plague - Book 1 is FREE:

The Alpha Plague - Available Now For FREE at www.michaelrobertson.co.uk

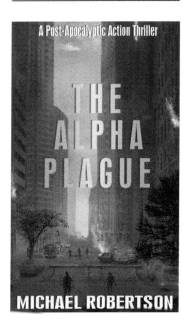

ABOUT THE AUTHOR

Like most children born in the seventies, Michael grew up with Star Wars in his life. An obsessive watcher of the films, and an avid reader from an early age, he found himself taken over with stories whenever he let his mind wander.

Those stories had to come out.

He hopes you enjoy reading his books as much as he does writing them.

Michael loves to travel when he can. He has a young family, who are his world, and when he's not reading, he enjoys walking so he can dream up more stories.

Contact
www.michaelrobertson.co.uk
subscribers@michaelrobertson.co.uk

ALSO BY MICHAEL ROBERTSON

~

New Reality: Truth

New Reality 2: Justice

New Reality 3: Fear

Sixth Cycle

Nuclear war has destroyed human civilization.

Captain Jake Phillips wakes into a dangerous new world, where he finds the remaining fragments of the population living in a series of strongholds, connected across the country. Uneasy alliances have maintained their safety, but things are about to change. -- Discovery **leads to danger.** -- Skye Reed, a tracker from the Omega stronghold, uncovers a threat that could spell the end for their fragile society. With friends and enemies revealing truths about the past, she will need to decide who to trust. -- Sixth **Cycle** is a gritty post-apocalyptic story of survival and adventure.

Darren Wearmouth ~ Carl Sinclair

DEAD ISLAND: Operation Zulu

Ten years after the world was nearly brought to its knees by a zombie Armageddon, there is a race for the antidote! On a remote Caribbean island, surrounded by a horde of hungry living dead, a team of American and Australian commandos must rescue the Antidotes' scientist. Filled with zombies, guns, Russian bad guys, shady government types, serial killers and elevator muzak. Dead Island is an action packed blood soaked horror adventure.

Allen Gamboa

Invasion Of The Dead Series

This is the first book in a series of nine, about an ordinary bunch of friends, and their plight to survive an apocalypse in Australia. -- Deep beneath defense headquarters in the Australian Capital Territory, the last ranking Army chief and a brilliant scientist struggle with answers to the collapse of the world, and the aftermath of an unprecedented virus. Is it a natural mutation, or does the infection contain -- more sinister roots? -- One hundred and fifty miles away, five friends returning from a month-long camping trip slowly discover that death has swept through the country. What greets them in a gradual revelation is an enemy beyond compare. -- Armed with dwindling ammunition, the friends must overcome their disagreements, utilize their individual skills, and face unimaginable horrors as they battle to reach their hometown...

Owen Ballie

Whiskey Tango Foxtrot

Alone in a foreign land. The radio goes quiet while on convoy in Afghanistan, a lost patrol alone in the desert. With his unit and his home base destroyed, Staff Sergeant Brad Thompson suddenly finds himself isolated and in command of a small group of men trying to survive in the Afghan wasteland. **Every turn leads to danger**

The local population has been afflicted with an illness that turns them into rabid animals. They pursue him and his men at every corner and stop. Struggling to hold his team together and unite survivors, he must fight and evade his way to safety. **A fast paced zombie war story like no other.**

W.J. Lundy

~

Zombie Rush

New to the Hot Springs PD Lisa Reynolds was not all that
welcomed by her coworkers especially those who were passed over
for the position. It didn't matter, her thirty days probation ended on
the same day of the Z-poc's arrival. Overnight the world goes from
bad to worse as thousands die in the initial onslaught. National
Guard and regular military unit deployed the day before to the north
leaves the city in mayhem. All directions lead to death until one
unlikely candidate steps forward with a plan. A plan that became an
avalanche raging down the mountain culminating in the salvation or
destruction of them all.

Joseph Hansen

~

The Gathering Horde

The most ambitious terrorist plot ever undertaken is about to be put
into motion, releasing an unstoppable force against humanity.
Ordinary people – A group of students celebrating the end of the
semester, suburban and rural families – are about to themselves in
the center of something that threatens the survival of the human
species. As they battle the dead – and the living – it's going to take
every bit of skill, knowledge and luck for them to survive in Zed's
World.

Rich Baker